Humbug

NINA BAWDEN

CLARION BOOKS

New York

Clarion Books
a Houghton Mifflin Company imprint
215 Park Avenue South, New York, NY 10003
Text copyright © 1992 by Nina Bawden

Printed in the USA

Library of Congress Cataloging-in-Publication Data

Bawden, Nina 1925–
Humbug / by Nina Bawden.
p.   cm.
Summary: When eight-year-old Cora is sent to stay next
door with the seemingly pleasant woman called Aunt Sunday,
she is tormented by Aunt Sunday's mean-spirited, deceitful
daughter, but finds an ally in Aunt Sunday's elderly mother.
ISBN 0-395-62149-6
[1. Honesty — Fiction.   2. Old age — Fiction.   3. Parent
and child — Fiction.   4. Self-reliance — Fiction]   I. Title.
PZ7.B33Hu   1992
[Fic] — dc20   91-33900
                                                              CIP
                                                              AC

BP 10 9 8 7 6 5 4 3 2 1

For Seth, Sam, Matthew, Timo, Ottilie, David, Jeremy, and Toby, a piece of advice, and for Perdita, a thank-you for the loan of her tramp.

Novels for Young Readers by Nina Bawden

CARRIE'S WAR
DEVIL BY THE SEA
THE FINDING
A HANDFUL OF THIEVES
HENRY
THE HOUSE OF SECRETS
KEPT IN THE DARK
THE OUTSIDE CHILD
THE PEPPERMINT PIG
REBEL ON A ROCK
THE ROBBERS
THE RUNAWAY SUMMER
SQUIB
THREE ON THE RUN
THE WHITE HORSE GANG
THE WITCH'S DAUGHTER

Humbug

⋅⋅∽ C H A P T E R ⋐⋅⋅

1

Alice and William and Cora lived with their mother and father, who were no better and no worse than most parents. Their father picked his nose when no one was watching, and since children are "no one" he picked his nose in front of them. Their mother told lies; she had given up smoking but sometimes when they came home from school the windows were wide open — even in winter, with a great icy gale tearing all through the house — and they knew she was hoping to get rid of the smell before anyone could come home and catch her.

Although their parents were not perfect, Alice and William and Cora were used to them and quite fond of them, and so they were sorry when their father told them that the bank was sending him to Japan for six months and he wanted to take their mother with him.

"Why can't we come?" asked Cora, who was eight, and

always asked the sort of questions that Alice and William, who were twelve and ten, knew there was no point in asking.

"All sorts of reasons, too many to go into just now," their father said, looking wise and grown-up.

"You mean you want to have a holiday without us," Cora said. (This was the sort of thing that Alice and William were too old to say.)

"Of course we don't, darling," their mother said.

But she had gone rather pink. William was sorry for her, being caught out, and so he said, quickly, "Why do you want to go to Japan?"

"The Japanese know more about banks than the rest of the world," their father said, and would have gone on, they could see, telling them boring things about money, if their mother had not stopped him.

She said, "You're going to stay with Granny and Grandpa, you'll like that, and you'll be going to school there at the end of the holidays. Japanese schools are very strict and if you came with us you would have to learn Japanese." She looked bright-eyed and pleased with herself as she produced this conclusive argument, and when Cora pulled one of her faces and said that she liked learning new languages, her mother just smiled, as if she knew better.

Alice and William and Cora were quite happy with this arrangement. Their grandmother and grandfather were on the whole less trouble to live with than their mother and father. They didn't fuss about the time children went to bed, nor insist that they ate what was good for them, and they didn't have dinner parties where everyone had too much to drink and got noisy. The only thing wrong with Granny and Grandpa's house was their disgustingly smelly old dog, who spent most of the time whimpering and dreaming on the only really comfortable sofa.

But when they arrived, the old dog was dead, and their grandmother had broken her leg.

They knew about the dog first because Grandpa met them at the station without him and Cora asked where he was. (Unlike Alice and William, she didn't mind old dog smells and had always been happy to curl up with him on his sofa.)

"He was very old, Cora," Grandpa said. "Seventeen. If you multiply by seven that will give you his age in human terms, which means he was a hundred and nineteen years old. So I daresay he was getting to feel pretty tired."

And then, because he could see that Cora was going to cry — or pretend to cry, anyway, because she thought he expected her to — he said, very quickly, "And I'm afraid your granny had an accident yesterday."

She had been climbing the apple tree in the back garden, Grandpa explained. "Too old for that sort of thing, but you can't change people at her age. And she didn't want me to tell your mother. No need to spoil the children's holiday just because I've been an old silly, she said. Meaning by children your mother and father, of course. Your grandmother thinks we can all manage if she has a bed downstairs and directs operations."

He snorted as if he didn't altogether believe this, and as they walked along with him, Alice and Cora on either side, holding his rough, red, cold hands, William thought he looked worried. He said, "Alice and I can cook, Grandpa. We do at home, sometimes. Cora hasn't started yet because she's not quite tall enough for the stove and there's a danger with boiling water. But Mother says it's a civilized skill all people should learn when they're young."

"That sounds like your mother," Grandpa said. "Making a virtue out of something that suits her."

"Your hand is shaking, Grandpa," Cora said. "Is that because you are old?"

She didn't wait for an answer. They had come to the cinder path that led to the last two houses in the road: Granny and Grandpa's house and the twin house next door. Cora dropped Grandpa's hand to run ahead and be first through the gate. She raced to the porch, shouting, "Granny, we're here," and hurtled through the open front door.

And stopped, just inside the sitting room. Granny was on the old sofa tucked up under a blanket. But she wasn't alone. There was a big man, who must be the doctor because he was holding her wrist and looking at his watch. And the tall woman standing beside him was looking at Cora in a way that made her face burn.

This woman said, "Goodness me, what a way for a nice little girl to rush into a sickroom. Didn't you know your poor Granny was ill?"

"It's all right, Sunday dear," Granny said. "I'm glad to see Cora."

But she sounded tired, and she looked smaller and paler than the children remembered.

She did her best to smile at them cheerfully. She said it was lovely to see them. She said she was sorry she had been such a silly. She said she was afraid they would have to look after Grandpa for a day or two because the doctor had decided she ought to go into hospital to have some more X rays. She introduced them to the tall lady, who had come to live next door and was called Sunday Dearheart, and said that "Aunt Sunday" would keep an eye on them all.

"Why is she called Sunday?" Cora asked. "That's the day of the week, not the name of a person."

"Perhaps you should ask her," Grandpa said. He made a strange, sudden noise — a sort of *humphing* sound at the back of his throat. William thought he was embarrassed, but it seemed to Alice that he was trying to stop himself laughing.

Sunday Dearheart looked pleased. She was a beautiful lady with shining brown hair piled high on her head, like a crown, and round, shining, blue eyes, and fat, shining red lips, and big, white, shining teeth. She said, "Monday's child is fair of face, Tuesday's child is full of grace — do you know the rest of the poem?"

Alice said, "I expect you were born on a Sunday." She spoke in a thoughtful voice, and Cora saw their grandmother look at her sharply.

Cora said, "Are you very ill, Granny? Are you going to die?"

Alice and William said, "Cora!"

The big doctor bellowed with laughter. He said, "Die? Your grandmother? If I'm any judge, she'll live to be a hundred!"

"Only if she promises not to be a naughty girl," Sunday Dearheart said, playfully wagging her finger at her friend on the sofa. "Climbing apple trees! A lady of your age ought to know better."

Cora giggled; she thought it was rather exciting to hear a grown-up being told off.

Her grandmother said, "What I don't know by now, Sunday dear, I'm unlikely to learn." She turned her head a little, so that Sunday Dearheart couldn't see her face, and winked at Cora. Then she said, in a soft, coaxing voice, "Aunt Sunday has a little girl who is just your age, Cora. Her name is Angelica. We thought it would be fun for you to have someone to play with, so Aunt Sunday has invited you to stay next door while I am in hospital. Isn't that kind of her?"

·∙·ᘓ C H A P T E R ᘓ·∙·

2

"I won't," said Cora. "I won't. I WON'T, I WON'T."
But even Cora knew there was no point in shouting. Grandpa had gone to the hospital, and only William and Alice could hear her. So she said in a lower voice, grumpily, "Grandpa doesn't have to look after me. I can take care of myself just like you."

"We know that," William said. "*They* don't, that's the trouble. Grown-ups don't. They think you're too young for an old man to look after."

William and Alice were washing up the breakfast dishes that Grandpa had left in the sink. They had had to throw away a carton of sour milk and a cabbage that had gone slimy inside. The whole kitchen smelled musty.

"I'll tell Mum and Dad when they ring," Cora said. "They're sure to ring from the airport to see if we got here all right. So I'll tell them what's happened, and they can tell Grandpa that it's all right for me to stay here with you."

"They've already rung." Alice looked very carefully at the dish she was drying instead of looking at Cora. She said, "You were upstairs in the lavatory. There was no time to call you because their flight was just boarding. William said you were fine. He said we all were."

Turning from the sink, looking over his shoulder, William saw Cora's eyes, black with anger. He said, "It's what Granny and Grandpa wanted. And even if I'd told Mum and Dad what had happened, they'd still have gone, wouldn't they? Only difference is, they'd have gone feeling miserable."

"I'm miserable now," Cora said crossly. "I suppose that doesn't matter."

"Mum and Dad are going to Japan," Alice said. "You're only going next door. You can see William and me whenever you want. Every day. And you know you hate housework. . . ." She folded her drying cloth, hung it neatly on the rail of the Aga oven, and smiled sweetly at Cora. "If you stayed here with us, you'd have to help Grandpa. You're not allowed to cook, so you'd get all the dull jobs. Peeling potatoes and scrubbing out saucepans. Even when Granny comes back from the hospital she won't be able to spoil you. And I expect that might worry her. She knows you expect her to make a big fuss of you, just because you're the youngest!"

"Oh, drop dead," Cora said. She thought she would like to kill Alice.

William knew how she felt. He didn't take her part against Alice. He never did. But he said, sympathetically, "This girl next door, this Angelica person, may be quite nice. You don't know."

"I expect she's called Angel for short," Cora said. "And I *do* know. I just know she'll be horrible."

Cora was right. Most of the time she was right about people.

Cora had guessed that Angelica would be horrible, and she was horrible. She had guessed that she would be pretty, and she was pretty. Angelica had soft, yellow hair, and soft, pink, pouting lips, and teeth that shone like pearls when she smiled. She was pretty, and strange-looking, too. Her eyes were different colors. One was a pale, pebbly brown with yellow flecks in it; the other was a sharp and glittering green. Like a piece of green glass. Or an emerald.

"This is Angelica, Cora," Aunt Sunday said. She spoke in such a hushed and respectful voice that Cora wondered if she were expected to curtsy.

She said politely, "How do you do? It's kind of you to ask me to stay, Angelica."

"We call her Angel for short," Aunt Sunday said. "That is, when she's good." She put her head on one side and smiled at Angelica. "But then you always are good, aren't you, dear heart?"

"Mother is making a joke," Angelica said in a disgusted voice. It seemed to Cora that the green eye snapped spitefully. She felt, suddenly, that it was as if there were two separate people inside Angelica: a not very nice but quite ordinary girl peeping out through the brown eye, and a much more unpleasant person, a kind of bad witch, perhaps, looking out through the green one.

Aunt Sunday said, "Not a very good joke, I'm afraid." She sounded apologetic. She gave a little cough and went on — changing the subject, Cora thought, as if she were afraid of Angelica — "Darling, why don't you take Cora upstairs. I'm sure she would like to see your pretty room."

Cora thought she would prefer to see where she was going to sleep. She hoped it would be the little room over the porch. She always slept in that little room when she stayed with Granny and Grandpa, and she knew that except for being the other way round, this house was exactly the same.

But it seemed that she was to sleep in Angelica's room, in the bottom bunk bed. "Just in case you wet yourself," Angelica said, looking sideways at Cora with her green, witch's eye. "I don't want your pee dripping down on me."

"Oh, I do something *much* worse than wetting my bed!" Cora said cheerfully. "I make a really horrible *noise*. I snore and I snuffle and I *grind my teeth*. My brother and sister say sleeping in the same room as me is like sleeping next to a rusty old engine. Or trying to sleep through an earthquake. So I always sleep by myself in the boxroom over the porch."

Cora smiled very sweetly. She said, "There's nothing I can do. I can't help it."

Angelica said, "My mother will be furious if you keep me awake. I don't know what she'll do to you but it'll be something awful. Fasten your mouth up with sticky tape. Or put you to sleep in the coal shed."

"Oh, dear," Cora said. "I don't think my grandpa would like that, do you? I expect he'd tell the police and they'd send your mother to prison for cruelty."

Angelica was frowning now. Flummoxed, Cora thought happily. Arguing with nasty people was more fun than just pinching and punching. She said, " 'Course, we could ask your mum if I could sleep in the boxroom. That's where I sleep next door, at my granny's."

Angelica's frown disappeared. She said, speaking slowly and thoughtfully, "Well, you could *ask*. I mean, there's no harm in *asking*. Old Ma Potter might not mind sharing her bed with you. And I don't suppose *you'd* mind her talking in her sleep, or screaming fit to wake the dead when she dreams someone is chasing her, not if you make a lot of noise, too. But Ma Potter makes horrible *smells*, and she has to have a chamber pot under the bed in case she needs to go in the night because Mother is scared she'll fall down the stairs if she goes to the bathroom."

Angelica's green eye was sparkling with triumph. Like an emerald in the sun, Cora thought. She said, in a pretending-to-be-bored voice, "Who on earth is Ma Potter?"

"Don't you *know*? She's *my* granny. She used to live in Underhill House, outside the town, in the country, but then she got too old to live by herself."

"Why do you call her Ma Potter?"

"It's what she *asked* to be called, stupid."

"Stupid yourself!" Cora was boiling up with rage suddenly, clenching her fists. She thought she would like to kill Angelica.

Angelica giggled. "Don't you *dare*. . . ."

Cora forced herself to keep still. She could feel her stomach muscles twitch with the effort. She said, "Well, I think you sound stupid, so there! All the silly names you have in your family. *Angel* and *Sunday*. As if you ought to be in the Bible. I suppose you think you're so wonderful you can't have ordinary names! Ma Potter, when she's your grandmother!" She snorted, and said something she had often heard her own grandmother say. "I've never heard such a thing. Not in all my born days."

"It's what she likes to be called," Angelica said. "She used to be a schoolteacher and when she was old and got to be a headmistress, she found out that the kids called her Ma Potter behind her back. But instead of being cross, she was pleased. She says she'd rather be called Ma Potter than Mother, or Granny. She says it makes her feel more of a real person. But *my* mother says she always was selfish and she hasn't got any better now she's grown old."

Cora wondered what Aunt Sunday had meant. She wondered if Ma Potter was older than her own grandmother. She decided that she must be, since her granny could not only look after herself but could still climb trees — even if she had just fallen out of one. She thought Ma Potter must be very small, too, to fit in the boxroom.

When *her* granny came to stay with them in London, she always slept in Alice's room, which was the second-best bedroom, and Alice moved in with William.

Cora said, "What about her clothes and things? I mean, *my* granny says that room's only a cupboard, not big enough to swing a cat."

"Old people don't need a big room." Angelica gave a sneery sort of laugh as if to say, "Don't you know *anything*?" Then she said, in a sweet, patient voice, like a silly grown-up talking to a young child, "She doesn't have many clothes; all she brought with her were a lot of old books and some old cups and saucers that she said mustn't go in the dishwasher. Well, my mother wasn't having *that*, was she? After all!"

Angelica sighed and rolled her eyes. Cora thought she really was the most horrible person she had ever met. Alice was horrible sometimes, but never as horrible as this. Angelica was so horrible that when she said, her green-witch, witch-green eye glinting, "I know your father had to go to Japan. But why didn't your mother stay at home to look after you?" Cora felt suddenly quite afraid of her. And afraid that if she answered Angelica, if she said anything at all, she would start to cry.

·꒓ C H A P T E R ꒐··

3

Cora didn't cry. She didn't talk, either. "You're very quiet, dear," Aunt Sunday said later on when they were sitting at the table in the big downstairs room, eating pasta for supper. "Don't you like your spaghetti? I can boil you an egg, if you'd rather."

Cora shook her head. The pasta was very good, with a lovely sauce of herbs and tomatoes, the kind of sauce she liked best. But when she wondered what Grandpa and Alice and William were having for supper next door, only on the other side of the wall, she felt too full in her chest to be hungry.

Angelica said, "I think she feels sad because her mother has gone away and left her. I know fathers have to go away sometimes, like my father does, but it's different for mothers."

Aunt Sunday said nothing. She seemed to be concentrating on her spaghetti, twisting the strands neatly around the prongs of her fork. When she glanced up, it was not at Angelica but at Ma Potter, who was sitting next to Cora, eating her pasta with a spoon and making rather a mess of it, sploshing red sauce on the white tablecloth.

It wasn't her fault, Cora saw. She was very old, older than Cora could have imagined; years and years older than Granny and Grandpa. Grandpa's hands shook sometimes, but Ma Potter could barely hold her spoon. She breathed with a rough, raspy sound as if each small breath hurt her; her eyes were pale and watery, with scaly pouches of skin hanging under them; and although her white hair sprouted strong and stiff on her chin, on her pink scalp it was thin as a veil, or a spider's web.

She looked very old and shabby. Out of place in this big living room, in which everything was glossy with newness, not a grubby mark or a speck of dust anywhere. Aunt Sunday and Angelica looked as if they had both just been washed and ironed and as if nothing could ever ruffle them or make them dirty. Even spaghetti and tomato sauce vanished neatly into their clean, rosy mouths. Not a spot left, not even on their fat, pink lips.

Angelica was looking at Cora's chin. She said, "You've got stuff all round your mouth, you're as bad as Ma Potter."

Cora expected Aunt Sunday to tell her not to be rude. But Aunt Sunday said nothing.

Angelica was smiling now. Smiling at her mother. She

said, "You wouldn't go away with my father, would you? Not unless you took me with you. You wouldn't ever leave *me* behind?"

"No," Aunt Sunday said. "I wouldn't want to leave my Angel."

"See, Cora?" Angelica said. Her eyes and her skin shone suddenly, as if they had been polished with excitement. "My mother wouldn't leave me and go to Japan. My mother loves me, that's why. Don't you, Mother?"

Cora thought this was the unkindest thing that had ever been said to her. She could hardly believe it. She felt her face go lumpy and solid with misery. She put her fork down and stared at her plate. Tears made it wobble in front of her.

"Of course I do, Angel darling," Aunt Sunday said. "And I'm sure Cora's mother loves her."

Angelica pouted and wriggled her shoulders. "Not as much as you love *me*. Or she wouldn't go off and leave her. You wouldn't go away and leave *me*."

Aunt Sunday laughed. "You know I wouldn't leave my little girl, Angel. Your father wouldn't want me to. He knows little girls need looking after."

It seemed to Cora that what they were saying was that neither her father nor her mother loved her, or they wouldn't have left her. She thought of sensible ways to answer. She hadn't been "left alone," because she had Alice and William. Her parents hadn't known what was going to happen. That Granny would break her leg, and that Cora would have to stay all by herself with these horrible people.

Ma Potter spoke. She said, in a low, growly voice, "Humbug."

She had spoken very quietly. Aunt Sunday, who was getting up, collecting plates, did not seem to have heard her. Nor did Angelica. Cora wondered if she had imagined it. Ma Potter was sitting bent over, head forward, eyes closed. She looked as if she might be asleep.

Aunt Sunday said, "I'm going to whip some cream to put on the raspberry fool. Angel dear, would you bring the dirty plates to the kitchen?"

When they had gone, Ma Potter opened her eyes. She said, "Pay no attention, child. Don't upset yourself. Just humbug, that's all."

"What do you mean?" Cora whispered.

Although Ma Potter didn't exactly whisper back, she didn't shout, either. And she was watching the half-open door as she spoke. As if, like Cora, she didn't want Angelica or Aunt Sunday to hear her. She said, "Oh, a lot of it goes on. Especially in this house, you'll find. Saying what sounds nice. What you want to believe. Not what's true. That's what she does all the time."

Cora wondered if she meant Angelica or Aunt Sunday. She said, "You mean, telling lies?"

"Not altogether. Humbuggery is what people talk without thinking. Lies are deliberate. Are you a clever child?"

"Yes," Cora said. "I can add up quite big sums in my

head, and I can read very well, all the books Alice can read, and she's twelve."

Ma Potter smiled. She didn't look quite so old when she smiled, Cora thought. It made her face look less baggy. Cora said, "Alice doesn't like me to tell people that. She says it sounds boastful."

Ma Potter gave a sudden, loud cackle. "If you decided it was more polite to pretend not to be clever, *that* would be humbug. Mind you, I daresay most people would like you more for it. Now in *her* case, my daughter Sunday's case, it's something else again. She'll persuade herself black is white if it suits her."

She was looking quite wide-awake now. But at that moment Aunt Sunday came back from the kitchen and, as she walked through the door, Ma Potter seemed to shrivel into a very old person again, folded over and dozy.

Aunt Sunday said brightly, "Have you been talking to Ma Potter, Cora? That's nice of you, dear." She put a glass bowl on the table; something pink and fruity, covered with spikes of whipped cream. "Poor old soul, life is a bit dull for her, I'm afraid." She raised her voice and shouted, "BRIGHTEN THINGS UP A BIT FOR YOU, WON'T IT, MA? HAVING CORA HERE."

Cora was surprised. When *she* had whispered, Ma Potter had heard her. But she didn't answer Aunt Sunday. She seemed to have gone to sleep.

"Deaf as a post," Aunt Sunday said. "Or deaf when she wants to be."

"Make her wait for her pudding," Angelica said. "Let's play the game, Mother."

What game? Cora saw Aunt Sunday shake her head at Angelica. A warning that Cora was not meant to see. Then she said, with a bright, toothy smile, "Sometimes we tease Ma Potter a little bit. Just for fun."

Angelica giggled. "Shall I tell you what we do, Cora? She's got such a sweet tooth, she's dreadfully greedy for puddings. So sometimes we teach her a lesson. She doesn't see very well. So we mix something up with her helping." She laughed, putting her hand over her mouth, spluttering, pink with excitement. "Salt," she said. "Once, I put a *dead fly*."

Cora felt sick. She said, "That's horrible. Yucky and beastly."

She looked at Aunt Sunday. She expected her to tell Angelica to apologize to her grandmother. Or to leave the table at once and go to her room. But Aunt Sunday was smiling as if she thought what Angelica had said was both clever and funny. Her blue eyes were shining as if a lamp was burning behind them.

She served the raspberry fool. She filled one bowl very full. She said, "Pass this to Ma Potter please, Cora."

Cora watched carefully. No salt. No dead fly. As she put the bowl down in front of Ma Potter she said, "It's all right. It looks very nice. A very nice pudding."

Both Angelica and Aunt Sunday laughed. Laughed and

laughed. Rocking backward and forward, holding their stomachs as if laughing so much was quite painful.

"She *believed* us!" Angelica gasped. "Isn't she *stupid!* I mean, we did warn her, we did tell her it was a game. Honestly, you are stupid, Cora!"

Cora sat silent. Hunched up, like Ma Potter. It seemed safer, somehow, not to move, not to speak. For the second time that day she felt suddenly frightened.

·❧ C H A P T E R ❧·

4

There was no need to be frightened, of course. Grandpa was next door, and Alice, and William. Just on the other side of the wall. She only had to shout and one of them would be able to hear her.

Cora could hear them. Grandpa's television, which he liked to have turned up fairly loud, and occasionally his voice rumbling on. And she heard Alice once, squealing in fun; Grandpa or William must be teasing her. Silly Alice, Cora thought. But she missed her. She wondered if Alice or William would come in to say good night. She remembered that she was supposed to take her medicine at bedtime to stop her grinding her teeth in her sleep. It hadn't worked yet, and she hated taking it because it was bitter, but Alice liked to remind her. Bossy Alice. Cora thought that she wouldn't mind Alice being bossy this evening.

But it was Grandpa who came. Cora had had her bath first, before Angelica, and was in her pajamas and ready for bed. She heard him from the top of the stairs and was down before he had stopped wiping his feet on the mat. "Hallo, pet," he said. "All hunky-dory?"

She opened her mouth, but Aunt Sunday answered for her before she could speak.

"Everything's fine," she said. "We're getting on beautifully, aren't we, Cora darling? I thought she was missing her mummy just a teensy bit to begin with, but she's been having such a lovely time with my dear little Angel I don't suppose she'll ever want to go home."

Cora was so shocked by this lie that she couldn't speak. She stood silent, her mouth hanging open.

Grandpa said, "You all right, pet? Not getting a cold, I hope."

"Oh, I do hope not," Aunt Sunday said. "I wouldn't want Angel to catch a cold. She catches things easily. She's so sensitive. Though of course, on the other hand, she is tremendously healthy. The doctor says she has a really wonderful constitution."

"I do understand," Grandpa said gravely. "Both delicate *and* strong. Hard to know which is more worrying."

Cora found her voice. She said, hopefully, "I do feel a bit sniffly." But before she could go on to say that it might be better if she went home with Grandpa, to sleep on her own in the little room over the porch, Aunt Sunday had whisked him down the hall to the living room and settled him next to Ma Potter, on a pink satin sofa.

Cora thought they both looked out of place on the pale, glossy cushions. Grandpa wasn't as old as Ma Potter, but he was just as shabby. The leather patches had worn off the elbows of his old gardening jacket, and his shoes were filthy; they had left muddy tracks on the soft, yellow carpet. And then he got out his smelly old pipe. He didn't light it, just sucked at it thoughtfully, but Cora was terrified he would suddenly take it into his head to start banging it on the side of his shoe and shake out the old tobacco and dottle. Although smoking was a disgusting habit, as she and Alice and William had often told Grandpa, Cora didn't want him to get into trouble with Aunt Sunday about it. There was no sign of an ashtray anywhere in this clean, tidy room. Cora stared at him hard, trying to will him into looking at her so that she could warn him somehow. But he was watching Aunt Sunday, who was busy rolling her round blue eyes at him and flashing her dazzling teeth.

She was asking him if he wanted supper, saying she knew how hungry he must be, telling him in almost the same breath that she was a very good cook, everyone said so. And it would be no trouble at all; once "the girls" were in bed, she would be delighted to prepare a meal for him, she had nothing else to do, apart from helping Ma Potter upstairs and settling her for the night. Or if he just wanted a quiet time to rest and recover, she would get him a hot milky drink, or perhaps "something stronger," and leave him *absolutely* alone, and in peace.

She was being really soppy, Cora thought. Stupid, too.

Grandpa hated to be fussed over. But although his ears had gone red, which showed he was a little embarrassed, he didn't seem to mind all that much: he had put his dirty old pipe away and was sitting up, very bright-eyed and straight-backed.

He said, "It's kind of you, Mrs. Dearheart, but I've got the other two children next door to be seeing to, and I promised to read to them."

"You promised you'd read *The Sword in the Stone* last time we came," Cora wailed. "You mustn't read it to Alice and William without me, it's not fair."

Grandpa looked startled, as if he had forgotten Cora was there. Aunt Sunday shook her head reproachfully. "That's not very nice, is it, Cora? Don't you think it's rather selfish of you to be thinking about yourself when your poor granny is ill and in hospital?"

Ma Potter laughed. She was sitting quite still at the other end of the sofa, her head on her chest, apparently fast asleep.

"Dreaming," Aunt Sunday flashed her teeth at Grandpa. "She sleeps most of the day now. Nothing else to do, the doctor says, she ought to get and about, but I say to him, the poor old thing has worked hard all her life, why shouldn't she sleep a bit at the end of it?"

She shook her head sadly.

"Is your mother so ill?" Grandpa asked, speaking softly, and leaning forward a little as if he thought Ma Potter might hear him. And, indeed, her eyes were only half closed; Cora could see the dark gleam between her cheekbones and eyelids.

"Just worn out," Aunt Sunday said. "She went on far too long, living alone in that big, old house that had belonged to her parents. Doing most of the work in an enormous garden. She said she loved it, she was always a contrary, pigheaded woman. But I could see it was much too much for her. So I kept on at her until she agreed to sell up and move in with me."

"Ah," Grandpa said. He was looking at Aunt Sunday in a funny, questioning way, as if he thought there was something wrong with what she had said. Cora didn't know what it could be, after all Aunt Sunday was taking care of Ma Potter, and that was a kind thing to do, wasn't it?

"Not that she thanks me for it," Aunt Sunday went on, with an indignant toss of her head. "Oh, no! I wait on her hand and foot, pay all the bills, wash her clothes, cook for her. All she has to do is eat the good food I put down in front of her. But if I had a hundred pounds for each time I had heard her say thank you, I wouldn't be a rich woman, believe me! Not by a long chalk!"

She was smiling at Grandpa as if she were making a joke. But her eyes were angry.

Grandpa was frowning.

Ma Potter spoke. "What's the time? Goodness me, I think I must have dropped off again." She yawned, patting her mouth with her hand and blinking her eyes — *acting* waking up, Cora decided. Pretending that she hadn't heard what Aunt Sunday had said. "How rude of me," she said. "I'm so sorry. Did I miss something?"

"*Humph.*" This was the noise Grandpa made when he was trying not to laugh. He said, "No, no, Mrs. Potter. We were just chatting about this and that, nothing important. I only came in for a minute to see how young Cora was getting on, say good night, that sort of thing. So that's that. Best be going, I suppose."

He clapped his hands on his knees and stood up. He gave a bit of a groan as if getting up was an effort, but when Cora ran to him, he swung her up in his arms all the same. She clung to him, locking her hands round the back of his neck, trying to tell him by squeezing him tight that she didn't want to stay with these people. But he didn't understand. He laughed and unfastened her arms, and put her down. He said, "You're getting too big to pick up. Or I'm getting too old."

Aunt Sunday laughed. "I think we are rather a spoiled little girl, don't you, Grandpa?"

"I'm not a *we*," Cora said crossly. "And he's not *your* grandfather."

"Don't be rude, pet," Grandpa said gently. He looked at Aunt Sunday. "Bed's the best place, I think. She's had a tiring day. Saying good-bye to her parents, a long train journey, and then all the excitement this end. . . ."

Cora was furious because he was apologizing for her. She said, "I don't want to go to bed. I'm not *tired.*"

She stamped her foot. She could see Grandpa frown.

And Aunt Sunday's face seemed to swell and grow red, an angry balloon, bobbing above her. Threatening her.

Ma Potter said, "You may not be tired, child, but I am. And I could do with some help up the stairs."

Angelica was still in the bathroom. "Oh, we all have to wait on her ladyship," Ma Potter grumbled as they passed the closed door. To begin with she had leaned heavily on Cora's shoulder, but once up the stairs, out of sight of Aunt Sunday, she had straightened up and stepped out quite briskly.

She paused at the door of her room and looked down at Cora. She said, "No need to be too sorry for yourself. Always someone worse off than you are. Look at me. I've got a life sentence."

"You're a grown-up," Cora said. "You don't have to stay where other people put you. You could go somewhere else if you wanted."

Ma Potter chuckled. She turned the handle of the door and beckoned to Cora.

The little room was so crowded with furniture that there was barely space for the two of them. Ma Potter had to turn sideways to squeeze between the narrow bed and a chest of drawers under the window. When she sat on the bed, her knees were squashed against the chest. She said, "Who wants to swing a cat, anyway? Not that I am an animal lover. But I respect them, which is more important."

Cora did not know how to answer this. Instead she said, "You've got a lot of books."

The shelves reached to the ceiling and the books were jammed tight on the shelves. There were books piled on the floor, on the chest of drawers, on the only chair, on the bed.

"Have you read them all?" Cora asked. "It must have taken years. About a hundred years, I should think."

"Not quite as long as that," Ma Potter said. "On the other hand, there are a few I haven't got around to just yet."

"You'll have to be quick if you're going to get them all done before you die," Cora said.

"Fair enough," Ma Potter said. "But I've not got much else to do, so perhaps I shall manage it."

It struck Cora that Ma Potter was talking like an ordinary person. She still looked old, but she didn't sound old.

She said, "Anything take your fancy, child? Help yourself. You won't find a book anywhere else in this house. I suppose Angelica has been taught to read. All I can say is I've seen no sign of it."

"I expect she reads in bed," Cora said. What she meant was that she hoped Angelica read in bed. Otherwise she might want the light out.

"I shouldn't count on it," Ma Potter said. "Have you got a flashlight? If you haven't, there's one in that top drawer. But I should wait until her ladyship's asleep. She'll complain if you don't. Summon her minion. Her mother. My daughter. Aunt Sunday, you call her."

She gave a loud snort. "Ridiculous."

Cora said, "What's a minion?"

"Servant. Slave. Helot. Drudge."

"Do you mean Angelica bosses her mother around?"

"You saw for yourself," Ma Potter said. "What have you got there?"

It was a small book, smaller than a paperback, and with a red cover made of very soft leather. The title was printed in gold.

"*The Jungle Book*," Cora read. "Is it a good story?" she asked Ma Potter.

"Try it. Kipling's out of fashion. That shouldn't worry you. Fashion is mostly humbug."

Cora said, "It was humbug Grandpa saying I was tired and ought to go to bed when he knew I was really just angry. And Aunt Sunday said she had to take care of you because she was worried about you. Because you couldn't take care of yourself. Was that humbug, too?"

"You could say so," Ma Potter said. "It's a useful word. Particularly in this house." She was quiet for a minute. Then she said, "In fact, you might find it a bit of a talisman. I expect you know what to say when people are just rude and silly. I. G. N. O. R. E. Well, *humbug* is better. Say it under your breath and you may find it makes things a bit easier. Think of it as a magic word."

Cora tried it out. "Humbug," she said. "Humbug." She liked the sound of it.

She said, "When shall I say it?"

"You'll find out," Ma Potter said. She looked closely at Cora. Judging her, Cora thought. Testing her. Then she gave a quick little nod as if what she saw pleased her. "Don't worry about it," she said. "When the time comes, you'll know. Off with you now, or they'll start wondering what we are up to. Then we'll both be in trouble."

·ᛰᴄCHAPTERᛰ·

5

Cora had expected that Angelica would be making a plan to tease and torment her. Something horrid in her bed, probably; something *dead*. A dead bird. On its back with its feet curled in the air and its beak open and dusty. Like *Who Killed Cock Robin*. Or perhaps something alive. A worm. Or a slug. Her toes curled at the thought of her bare feet pushing down under the covers and meeting the cold dead thing, all stiff and bony, or the cold *living* thing, wriggly and squelchy.

Whatever it was, she would pretend not to care. I. G. N. O. R. E. No point in wasting *humbug* on a bit of nastiness in the bed. Magic was something you had to be sparing with. It might lose its power if you used it too often, or carelessly. As long as she had the idea of *humbug* hidden away in her mind she was safe. She thought — Like a secret weapon.

She wondered what else Angelica might have put in her bed. It wouldn't be anything ordinary, a prickly hairbrush or a damp facecloth. A person who could think of dropping dead flies in her grandmother's pudding had a disgusting mind. She would think of something disgusting. Like sick. Or worse. . . .

Standing on the landing, outside the bedroom she was to share with Angelica, Cora felt her stomach begin to heave. She said, under her breath, "I. G. N. O. R. E."

And pushed open the door.

The bottom bunk was neat and inviting. The duvet was folded back, showing the smooth white sheet underneath. And Cora knew she had been stupid to imagine Angelica would do anything so boring and obvious as make a mess in her bed.

Then she saw Angelica. She was standing close beside the wall that divided the two houses. She was holding a glass tumbler. She had put the open top of the tumbler against the wall, and her ear against its bottom.

Cora said, "What are you doing?"

She knew she shouldn't have spoken. She should have said nothing. Just got into bed and opened her book. As if she thought that holding a glass tumbler between your ear and the wall was perfectly normal behavior. I. G. N. O. R. E.

But Cora couldn't help asking. She was naturally an inquisitive person. And, of course, Angelica knew it.

Angelica giggled. She said, "Don't you *know?*"

"I wouldn't have asked if I did," Cora said.

Angelica giggled again.

Cora stared at her coldly. "You don't have to tell me," she said. "I don't *care*. I was just being polite. I mean, if I hadn't asked, it would only have been because I thought you'd gone mad. I was being *nice*, really. But I don't mind. You can stand there all night holding the wall up with that stupid glass if you want to. See if I care!"

"I'm not holding the wall up," Angelica said. "I'm listening."

Cora wondered if Angelica really was mad. She said cautiously, "Do you mean you're pretending? I used to do it with the chain on the door. Pretend it was a telephone. But that was a long time ago when I was a baby."

Angelica took the glass from the wall and shook her head wonderingly. "Don't you know *anything*?"

Then she smiled very nicely, as if she had suddenly made up her mind to be friends, and held the glass out to Cora. "Come on," she said, "try for yourself. You can hear through the wall."

Cora took the glass. She felt nervous and clumsy. She put the top of the glass against the wall and the bottom end against her ear. Angelica watched her. Her green eye was sparkling.

Cora heard Alice say, "Have you cleaned your teeth, William?" Her voice seemed very close. It made Cora jump.

She said, "Alice!"

Angelica laughed. "She can't hear you, stupid! Not unless she's got a glass, too. And I don't suppose she'd know how to use it. Nobody seems very bright in your family."

Cora said, "I can hear William talking but not what he's saying."

"That's because he's on the other side of the room now. By the door. I could hear him before." Angelica smiled — not a nice smile this time. She said, "*Everything* he was saying. And your sister, too."

Cora said, "That's sneaky!" Once she had said it she saw just how sneaky it was. She said, "It's a rotten, mean thing to do. Spying on people!"

She put the glass down on the chest of drawers and got on the bottom bunk bed. She lifted up the whole of the duvet, just to be sure there was nothing hidden beneath it, then settled it over her knees and sat with *The Jungle Book* on her lap.

"Goody-goody," Angelica said unpleasantly. "Bet you'd like to know what they said to each other. What they said about *you*. But I'm not going to tell you."

She climbed to the top bunk. She bounced around, getting settled, creaking the springs. Then she said, "I'm going to put the light out, but there's a switch on the wall for your bedside light if you want to read. I don't mind if you do."

The light went off. Cora felt for the switch and turned on a small spot. She opened *The Jungle Book* and closed it again. She turned off the spotlight and lay straight and still. She wondered what Alice and William had been saying about her. She wanted to know — and she didn't. She listened to Angelica breathing above her. Was she going to sleep?

She said, "Angelica. . . ."

Angelica said, "Alice said she was glad you were staying next door. She said it was dreadfully boring having to look after a little sister. She said she wished you had never been born."

She stopped. The darkness and silence pressed down on Cora. Her ears were throbbing.

Angelica went on, speaking slowly and softly. "Then William said that your mother and father hadn't wanted you either. They tried to give you away but everyone sent you back. You were so titchy and ugly. And you made those terrible noises at night. Grinding your teeth."

Cora felt as if she were suffocating. She said, gasping for air, "Little babies don't have teeth."

"Other noises, then," Angelica said. "Snoring and snuffling. Alice said your parents would have put you into an orphanage, except that they would have had to pay for you because you weren't really an orphan. And they couldn't afford it. So I suppose they just hoped you would die."

Cora said, "Alice never said that! Alice can't bear things to die. Not even *flies*." Or small, ugly babies.

"No, she didn't say it. I made that up. I was just being horrid. I'm sorry." Angelica sounded sorry. But she went on, all the same, "Everything else was true. Every bit. Though I suppose I shouldn't have told you. It was really unkind."

Cora said nothing. Angelica went on in a thoughtful voice, "I wish I could take it back. But I won't tell you any more. Nothing else that they said." She waited for Cora to answer her. When she didn't, Angelica said, coaxingly, sweetly, "So we can be friends now, can't we?"

Cora swallowed. Her mouth and her throat were dry. She licked her lips to moisten them. Just the thought of asking Angelica anything made her feel sick. But she had to know. She said, "What else did they say?"

Angelica said, reproachfully, "I said I was sorry about being unkind. I'm not going to be unkind *again*. I told you. I want to be friends."

"Friends tell each other everything," Cora said.

She crossed her fingers. Angelica could never be her friend, not if they were the only two people on a desert island, not in a hundred years.

"You won't like me if I do tell you," Angelica said.

"Yes, I will." Cora crossed all the fingers she could manage against this huge lie. She said, "I promise."

Angelica sighed. "You have to say *please*."

"Please."

"Just remember you *made* me. That I didn't want to."

"All right." Cora pulled her sick-cat face — slitting her eyes and wrinkling her nose and making a pinched, angry hole of her mouth.

Angelica said, "If it hadn't been for you, your mother

and father would have taken Alice and William to Japan with them. But William said he heard your parents talking and your mother said, *I've got to get away from that dreadful child Cora or I'll go stark staring mad.* And your father said, *I know just how you feel, my dear heart.*"

"That's your name!" Cora said. "My father calls my mother darling."

She was almost sure now that Angelica was making it up. But not quite sure, not absolutely. . . .

Angelica said, very sadly and sorrowfully, "I don't suppose I've got every word right *exactly.* Or perhaps William got one or two wrong. Like in Chinese Whispers. And I really *hated* having to tell you. I always hate telling people nasty things about themselves. It makes me feel as if I were crying inside me."

Cora wanted to laugh. If anyone enjoyed telling people horrible stories it was Angelica!

Ma Potter had said, "When the time comes, you'll know."

And Cora did know. She put her hand over her mouth and said the magic word very softly.

But not quite softly enough. Angelica said suspiciously, "What did you say, Cora?"

Cora smiled. "Just *good night*, Angelica."

"I slept like a top," Cora said, when Aunt Sunday asked her next morning at breakfast if she had been comfortable in her bunk bed.

She smiled at Angelica, who was watching her with a puzzled expression. Cora said, "I just hope I didn't keep Angelica awake, grinding my teeth. I always sleep well. Granny says it's because I have a clear conscience."

"Poor Granny!" Aunt Sunday said. "I'm afraid she didn't have such a good night. You haven't asked how she is, Cora. Had you forgotten she is in hospital?"

"I wouldn't have forgotten if it was poor old Ma Potter," Angelica said, very smugly.

Cora wished that Ma Potter was having breakfast with them instead of on a tray in her bed. She would know what Cora was silently saying. "Humbug," Cora said, in her mind. And, aloud, "I was going to ask Grandpa after breakfast."

"He's already gone to visit her," Aunt Sunday said. "He asked me to tell you what's happened." She paused, hoping, Cora saw, that she would think what had happened to Granny was terrible. And she was frightened, of course, though not so much as she would have been if Aunt Sunday had been a more ordinary person. She was like Angelica, Cora decided. It made her happy to frighten people.

Aunt Sunday said, "Your grandmother had an operation last night. The surgeon decided to put a pin in her leg to hold the bones together."

What sort of pin? It must be a safety pin, Cora thought. She said, "Did it hurt her?"

Angelica rolled her eyes, sniggering. "They put her to sleep, silly-billy. Don't you know about operations?"

"I had grummets in my ears when I was a baby," Cora said. "And William broke his arm playing football. But it mended when they put a cast on. No one pinned it."

Aunt Sunday said, "It's not quite so simple when you are an old lady, Cora. Granny may have to stay in hospital quite a while."

Cora understood what that meant. So did Angelica. Her witch-green eye flashed a triumphant and spiteful message at Cora. Then she said to her mother, in a put-on, sweet voice, "Cora will have to stay with us, won't she? Oh, I'm so pleased! She can be my best friend, not just in the holidays, but when I go back to school. She can be my bestest best friend all next term!"

It sounded like a prison sentence to Cora. She waited for Aunt Sunday to tell her how lucky she was that Angelica wanted to be her best friend and was surprised to hear her say, rather timidly, "You may not be going back to that school, Angel darling."

Cora had been staring glumly at the table. Now she looked up and saw that Angelica had gone very white. She said, "But I *want* to go back. I told you, Mother. You said you'd talk to my teacher. You promised!"

Aunt Sunday said meekly, "I did try. I'm sorry, my precious."

Angelica was scowling. She said, "You'd better try again, hadn't you? If I can't go back to that school, I won't go to another school ever! I'm bored with changing about just because some girls are so stupid!"

Aunt Sunday looked at her sadly. "I know, my poor darling. I feel the same about moving house. Such a wrench, always."

Until now, Cora had thought that Angelica looked simply upset, just as anyone might if something had gone wrong at school. But now, suddenly, she looked different; crafty and mean and much older. She said, "If they won't have me back, then I won't stay here in this house any longer."

Aunt Sunday gave a little gasp — as if someone had stuck a pin in her, Cora thought. She glanced slyly at

Cora as if she hoped she hadn't noticed how nasty Angelica had been to her.

I. G. N. O. R. E., Cora said to herself. And, to Aunt Sunday, "May I get down? I don't want any more breakfast. I need to go and see my brother and sister."

Angelica was off her chair before Cora had finished her sentence. "I'm coming with you."

Cora looked at Aunt Sunday. "I'm not going to play. It's just that, I *need* Alice. I want to write to Mum and Dad in Japan and I need her to help me with spelling."

She crossed her fingers under the tablecloth. She could spell almost as well as Alice. And better than William.

Angelica wailed at her. "You said you'd be my *friend*."

Aunt Sunday said, "And I'm sure she meant it, my darling." She turned a bright smile on Cora. "You mustn't be selfish, dear. My poor Angel doesn't have any brothers and sisters. She's sharing her home and her mummy with you, so you must share Alice and William."

Alice said, "We're not writing to Mum and Dad until Grandpa says. We don't want to worry them about Granny."

"When is she coming home?" Her grandmother would understand, Cora thought. Not like Alice and William, who were busy cleaning the kitchen as a surprise for Grandpa when he came back from the hospital. Granny would always stop what she was doing when Cora wanted to talk to her.

Cora said, "I need to see Granny. I could go with Grandpa to see her next time he goes."

Angelica could hardly expect to go to the hospital. Although Cora couldn't even be sure of that. Angelica was standing in the doorway of the kitchen, arms folded, eyes watchful. Cora thought — Guarding me! Like a policeman!

William said, "Grandpa says Granny's not well enough to see children yet, Cora. But you can write a letter to Mum and Dad if you want to. Then we can send it when Granny comes home."

"She says she needs Alice to help her with spelling," Angelica said.

Alice rolled her eyes up, hunched her shoulders, and sighed. She pulled the corners of her mouth down. Then, just in case Angelica might not understand what she meant by this brilliant act, she decided to speak. "Whatever is the child *talking* about? When did Cora ever ask anyone how to spell anything?"

"I wouldn't ask you to spell *anything*," Cora said. "That's an easy word."

"Oh, you're so sharp you'll cut yourself," Alice said nastily. She got up, pushed the newspapers and plastic bags back into the cupboard with her foot, and shoved the door shut. She had made the muddle worse, not better, Cora thought, but decided not to say so.

Alice knew what she was thinking all the same. It made her angrier still. "You tidy up if you think it's so simple, Miss Too-Clever-by-Half. Why do you tell silly lies? You're always swanking about how well you read, how well you write, how good you are at spelling!"

Behind Cora, Angelica laughed. Cora looked at her feet. She was wearing an old pair of Alice's sandals; her washed-out jeans, already too short for her, had once belonged to William. Perhaps Angelica had been telling the truth. Everyone hated her. Her parents made her wear her brother's and sister's old clothes. Alice and William said cruel things behind her back. They all wished she had never been born.

William said, "Maybe she wanted something else and didn't like to say."

He sounded so kind, Cora wanted to cry. But she must try not to cry in front of Angelica because that was what Angelica wanted. And she couldn't tell William anything important either, not while Angelica was standing behind her.

So she just went on staring at her feet in Alice's old sandals. She said — very low, almost whispering — "I want to go home. I mean, if Granny's not coming back from the hospital to look after me here, I want to go home."

Alice snapped at her. "Well you can't, Cora. Don't be childish."

"She can't help being childish, if she is a child," William said. He grinned at Alice, to show he was making a joke, not disagreeing with her. "Of course she mustn't be silly. But I expect she feels a bit lonely."

"I didn't think she was lonely," Angelica said. "I thought she was having a nice time with me."

Cora looked at her then. Angelica's lower lip was caught between her pearly teeth, and her pretty face was flushed and sad.

William said, "Oh, I'm sure she is, *really*. I mean . . ."

"She wants us to pity her. She likes attention, that's all," Alice said briskly. "Come on, Cora, be sensible. You've got a nice girl your own age to play with. . . ."

"She's not *nice*. SHE'S A SPY," Cora shouted.

The blood throbbed in her ears. They were all staring at her. William was trying not to smile. Alice's face was pink and cross. And Angelica — well, the way Angelica looked at her made Cora shiver. Her witch eye was glowing. Cora thought — Like a death ray.

But neither William nor Alice seemed to notice. They said, together, "Oh, *Cora!*"

Angelica's voice was soft and said. "I thought she liked me. I let her have the bottom bunk even though I hate sleeping on the top one. And she promised she'd be my friend."

Alice and William said, "Cora!" again. Then William said, "Don't be upset, Angelica! I'm sure Cora wants to be friends with you. She just gets silly sometimes. Says things she doesn't mean."

Cora thought — Traitor!

Alice said, "Why don't I get Grandpa's humbug jar down from the cupboard and give you one each? Grandpa's humbugs are special, you know that, Cora, don't you? When I was little, I used to think they were magic because he always gave me one when I hurt myself and it always made me feel better."

A little gate in the hedge led from one house to the other: it had been put there years ago when Granny's old aunt had lived where the Dearhearts lived now. Angelica went through first and Cora followed her slowly, sucking her humbug and thinking of magic. She thought she did feel a bit better.

But not for long. Angelica said, "Shut the gate properly behind you," and her voice wasn't soft and sweet but sharp, like a piece of ice cracking. Then she said, "If you ever do that again, if you tell on me, you'll be sorry. I'll put a hex on you."

···⁊CHAPTER⁊···

7

I t seemed to Cora that she was Angelica's prisoner just as much as if she had been locked in a dungeon.

Angelica would never let Cora be alone with Alice and William. Once or twice Cora thought she had escaped, but before she could open the little gate in the hedge that led to her grandparents' garden, Angelica was following close behind her. And when Grandpa came to Aunt Sunday's house to kiss Cora good night, Angelica was always there before he had rung the bell, waiting just inside the front door, ready to smile her sugary smile and talk in the sugary voice that made Cora want to throw up but seemed to please Grandpa. He took to patting Angelica on the head and calling her his "chickadee," or his "moppet," in a way that made Cora quite jealous. Angry, too. It was stupid of Grandpa to think that Angelica was a nice girl, when Cora knew that she wasn't.

Not that in the next few days Angelica did anything to Cora that was much more than teasing or spiteful; laughing behind her hand when Cora talked to Ma Potter about Mowgli and the wolves as if it was unbelievably stupid of Cora to be interested in someone who was only a character in a book, or waiting for Cora outside the lavatory and holding her nose and pretending to faint when she came out of it. But these were just things that some ordinarily silly girls did, and Cora began to feel, not happy or comfortable, but at least not too afraid of Angelica.

Besides, she wouldn't have to put up with her very much longer. Aunt Sunday had taken them both to see Granny in hospital, and although Angelica had pranced around swirling the red skirt of her pretty dress and making sure everyone noticed her, Granny had managed to wink at Cora privately. She wasn't impressed by a silly miss who had put on a party frock just to show off in front of an old lady in hospital! But the best thing about the visit was that Granny looked pink-cheeked and cheerful and quite spry on her crutches and said she would be home very soon. She said, "I'm afraid you'll have to move back next door, Cora darling. I'm sure you'll miss Angelica, and Aunt Sunday's good cooking, but this poor old cripple is going to need you!"

Cora thought the only thing she would miss would be Ma Potter's library. Although Granny and Grandpa had books in their house, they were not interesting to Cora. Granny's books were all about someone being found murdered and a policeman working out who had done it, and they made Cora feel queasy. She didn't like stories about blood and death. Grandpa read books about the First and the Second World Wars, which were also about killing (though different, of course, being history), but Grandpa said they were a bit long and dull for people of Cora's age.

Ma Potter had poetry books on her shelves, and books about traveling through deserts and jungles, and adventure books about exploring the Arctic Circle, and climbing mountains, and books for children, and books for grown-ups, and books (of the best kind, Ma Potter said) that were for just everyone. Some of these Cora had read, like *The Wind in the Willows* and *Stig of the Dump* and *The Peppermint Pig*, but she had never read anything by Rudyard Kipling before, and Ma Potter said that when she had finished *The Jungle Book* she might start on *Kim*. And to please herself as well as Cora, Ma Potter read the *Just So Stories* aloud.

Cora particularly liked "The Cat that Walked by Himself." But the best thing about Ma Potter reading to her was that Angelica got bored very quickly and went away, leaving Cora and Ma Potter sitting comfortably together on the sheltered veranda at the back of the house. Angelica never left Cora alone with anyone else. Not even with her own mother.

Cora liked to talk to Ma Potter about other things besides books. She told her about Alice and how cross she got when Cora argued with her, even when Cora was right about something. Just like some of the bigger girls at school, even some of the teachers. Ma Potter said that it was always hard on people to be told they were wrong by someone much younger, especially if the younger person was right.

And Cora liked to listen, too. Ma Potter told her about the olden days when she was Cora's age, and when Cora told her that Grandpa was interested in the history of old battles, she told her what had happened to her during the Second World War. She had been living with her husband and her baby (who was Aunt Sunday now) in a town called Coventry when the Germans bombed it and destroyed the cathedral. They destroyed Ma Potter's house in the same air raid, and Ma Potter and her husband and baby were trapped in the ruins. Ma Potter had found a stick and managed to poke a hole up through the rubble so there was fresh air to breathe, and she had hunched herself over the little baby to keep the stones and dust off her. She had stayed like that for two days, and by the time the rescue workers found them, Mr. Potter was dead. "I couldn't see him," Ma Potter said. "Though I could hear him calling me. I kept calling back, telling him to keep his spirits up, but I daren't try to reach him, even though he was no more than an arm's length away. I couldn't move, because of the baby. Everything would have come down on her. She would have been buried alive."

Cora thought of Ma Potter, crouching over her baby, making a bridge of her body to keep her from dying. And her poor husband calling to her to help him. She wondered if Ma Potter had sometimes wished she had tried to save her husband instead of Aunt Sunday. She could have had another baby. A baby was easier to replace than a husband. And the new baby would have had a father as well as a mother. Cora was sure Ma Potter would answer her if she asked, but then she decided that some people would think it was a rude question. Alice and William would say it was rude, certainly.

So instead she said, "What about Angelica's father. Did he die, too?"

"Gracious me," Ma Potter said. "What put that into your head? Oh yes, George Dearheart is alive, all right, though he keeps away, and I can't say I blame him. I daresay he'd like to cut loose altogether, but they've got their hooks into him."

She stopped. Angelica was there suddenly, standing in front of them. She must have come through the back door very quietly — *creeping up on them,* Cora thought, *listening.*

But all Angelica said at that moment was, "Mother says lunch is ready."

They had roast lamb with peas and potatoes and rhubarb and cream afterward. When it was finished, and Ma Potter had gone for her afternoon nap, Angelica said to her mother, "May I show Cora your jewels? I'm sure she would like to see them."

"Oh, I don't know," Aunt Sunday said. "Not all little

girls like to look at beautiful things quite as much as you do, my Angel."

Cora thought she knew what Aunt Sunday meant. Cora wasn't pretty, not like Angelica, and she didn't have pretty clothes to wear every day, only Alice's and William's old castoffs. How could such an ugly and badly dressed child possibly care about pretty jewelry?

Cora said, "I like diamonds. Real, sparkly diamonds. When I'm all dressed up to go to a party, my mother lets me borrow her big diamond ring. It's got an enormous, a really *huge* diamond in the middle, and lots of little ones round the edge. And rubies and emeralds, too."

Aunt Sunday laughed. "Oh, Cora! How could you keep one of your mother's rings on your little fingers?"

"I do so. I wear it on my thumb," Cora said stubbornly. But she knew Aunt Sunday didn't believe her.

"We'll be very careful," Angelica said in a coaxing voice. "Won't we, Cora?"

So Aunt Sunday fetched her jewel box, and told them to put everything back as they found it, and went upstairs to rest, like Ma Potter. She called it "having a bit of a lay down," and it surprised Cora that Aunt Sunday should want to sleep after lunch like a very old person. But Angelica seemed to think it was nothing out of the ordinary. She said, "I knew she'd let us play with her jewels if I asked now. Anything for a bit of peace and quiet in the afternoon."

The jewel box was made of brown leather with a rounded lid and gold bits at the corners to make it look like a treasure chest. Inside, there was a tray on the top, lined with velvet, and three drawers below, with gold knobs. There were little silk pockets on the underside of the lid. "Those are for earrings," Angelica said, taking out a pair of tiny silver bells that tinkled as she shook them. "I can't wear them because I haven't got holes in my ears, and my father says I mustn't have my ears pierced till I'm ten years old. He's going to buy me some gold bells for my tenth birthday."

She didn't look at Cora as she said this. She put the silver bells back and opened one of the drawers. "Of course most of her jewelry came from my father, he's always bringing wonderful things back from his travels. He goes traveling all over the world. But these old things are Ma Potter's. They used to belong to her mother and grandmother."

There was a necklace of moonstones and earrings to match, several plain and solid gold rings, a brooch made of silver filigree with green stones that changed color as the light moved about them, and a lot of shiny black jet.

"All these things will be mine, when Ma Potter dies," Angelica said. "And she's old, so I expect she'll die soon."

Although Cora knew this was probably true, she was embarrassed to hear Angelica talk about her grandmother's death in quite such a calm and cold tone. To change the subject, she said, "What does your father do when he travels? Is he an explorer? Or does he work in a bank like my father?"

"I am afraid I can't tell you what he does." Angelica

glanced over her shoulder as if she was afraid someone might come in and hear her and said, very low, "He works for the government. It's very secret work and very important. That's why he doesn't come home very often and why we sometimes have to move house in a hurry. He doesn't want to put us in danger in case we are kidnapped and made into hostages."

While she was saying this, she watched Cora closely. Cora wondered if she were telling the truth. She said, "If it's a really big secret, you ought not to tell me."

Angelica frowned, as if this was something she hadn't thought of. Cora said, "It's all right, I won't tell."

Angelica was still frowning. She said, "You'd better *swear.*"

Cora licked her finger and drew it across her throat. "See that wet, see that dry, cut my throat if . . ."

"No, I mean swear on the Bible!" Angelica got to her feet. "I've got a Bible Ma Potter gave me upstairs, I'll go up and get it."

She was looking very hot and excited suddenly, Cora thought. Nervous, too — as if there were something unusual and rather frightening in what she was about to do. Cora thought swearing on a Bible was stupid, since either you meant what you said or you didn't, but it wasn't all that scary or strange and she didn't mind doing it if that was what Angelica wanted.

Angelica didn't come back straightaway, and Cora began to get bored. She opened the bottom drawer of the jewel box and found it full of rings. Some of them had colored stones. There was a cloudy blue one with flecks of brown in it that she thought was especially pretty. And a big, single diamond that flashed when she put it on and twiddled it round on her finger. Like a lighthouse, she thought.

Then she heard Angelica coming back, making a lot of noise — *thump, thump,* as she jumped down the last of the stairs. Cora took the diamond ring off her finger and put it back with the others and closed the little drawer quickly. She had done nothing wrong. But she felt uncomfortable. She sat back on her heels and put her hands in her lap.

Angelica burst in, flinging the door wide, and looked at Cora. She smiled — not at her, Cora thought, but at something she was privately thinking. Then she said, "Sorry, couldn't find the old Bible anywhere. Never mind, I believe you. You bored with the silly old jewel box? I know I am, I'll take it up to my mother."

And she pounced on the small treasure chest, slammed the lid shut, tucked it under her arm, and ran out of the room and up the stairs again.

·❦ C H A P T E R ❧··

8

Angelica had an appointment with the dentist. She made a great fuss at breakfast next morning, sighing and rolling her eyes and pretending to be struck dumb with terror, as if she were about to have all her teeth pulled without anesthetic instead of just a routine inspection. Cora thought — Tragedy Queen! She was afraid that Angelica would want her to witness the rest of the drama and insist that Aunt Sunday take them both to the dentist, but Ma Potter, who had unexpectedly got up for breakfast, said that she was going out and would like Cora's company.

"What on earth *for?*" Aunt Sunday was looking annoyed, as if Ma Potter had somehow insulted her.

"Do you mean why do I want to go out? Or why I would like to take Cora?" Ma Potter smiled cheerfully. "I want to go out because there are certain things I wish to do, and I would like Cora with me in case I need help. I have ordered a taxi." It was the first time Cora had heard Ma Potter speak so firmly to Aunt Sunday. She thought that Ma Potter must have made up her mind to be brave before she got up this morning. She had dressed herself in a tweed jacket and skirt and a blouse with a bow at the neck and proper shoes with heels instead of her usual shapeless dress and old slippers. She didn't look smart, but she wasn't shabby. And although she had put too much powder on her face so that her big nose looked as if it had been dusted with flour, the proud and determined way that she lifted her chin as she spoke made her seem younger and stronger.

Aunt Sunday said in a terrible voice, "You know what the doctor said! And if you wear yourself out it won't be you who will suffer. Not you, oh no! You know what you are! You'll take to your bed and expect me to wait on you hand and foot!"

She sounded so angry, Cora felt her heart thump. And Angelica was watching her grandmother with a sly smile, as if she were eagerly awaiting her turn to be rude and unkind to her. Even though Cora told herself that Angelica was only a little girl, and couldn't really do anything to harm a grown person, that smile made her even more alarmed for Ma Potter.

"I thought the doctor told you I ought to get around a bit more," Ma Potter said. She was still smiling, if not quite so cheerfully. "Better to wear out than rust out, that's what people say, isn't it? And now I've got this nice child to go with me, I thought I would take the opportunity to have a look round the town, perhaps even go to the library. Not the kind of excursion either you or Angelica care for. Shall we go, Cora?"

The cab was waiting outside in the road, a big, black, old-fashioned cab, so beautifully polished that Cora could see herself in it. The driver was old, too, and when he took off his uniform cap, his bald head shone like his taxi. He said, "Good to see you again, Mrs. Potter. It's been a long time."

"Too long," Ma Potter said. "Let me introduce this young lady. Cora, this is Mr. Hughes, who has been a good friend of mine a long time. Mr. Hughes, this is Cora."

"How d'you do, miss," Mr. Hughes said. He took Cora's small hand in his large one and shook it politely.

They got into the taxi. Mr. Hughes climbed into the driver's seat and opened the glass panel between them. "Where to, my lady? Buckingham Palace?"

"Not today, Mr. Hughes. I believe Her Majesty is in Windsor Castle, so it would be a wasted journey."

Mr. Hughes laughed and thumped his hand on the steering wheel as if this was a brilliant joke, and Ma Potter winked at Cora. She said, "Underhill, if you please, Mr. Hughes. It's still empty, you know."

"All shut up, boards over the windows, front door chained and padlocked. You can't get in. Why upset yourself?"

"It's the Folly I had in mind," Ma Potter said. "I've still got a key for the Folly."

Mr. Hughes sighed. "Okay, okay. Have it your own way. You pay the piper. You call the tune."

He started the engine and they set off up the lane that led to the main road. When they got to the junction, they turned right instead of left to the station and the town. Cora said, "I thought we were going to the library?"

Ma Potter shook her head. "That was just to throw her off the scent," she said. "Though we might go to the library another day. Once I've tasted freedom, who knows?" She raised her voice so that Mr. Hughes could hear. "Nice to be out on parole. I've been in solitary confinement these last months."

"She said you'd gone down a lot when I asked her outside the Post Office," Mr. Hughes said. "I had it in mind to pay you a visit, but she gave me the brush-off. Far too poorly for company was what she said."

"Oh, she would. She'd have me in leg irons if she dared."

Cora supposed that "her" and "she" meant Aunt Sunday. But the conversation seemed mysterious to her. She decided that Ma Potter and Mr. Hughes had a private language between them and there was no point in listening.

She looked out of the window. They were out in the country now, driving through narrow lanes with high hedges. From time to time they passed a farm gateway and Cora saw fields sweeping up; yellow cornfields, green pasture. They passed a church with a round tower on the edge of a village that was just a few cottages and a duck pond. They had to wait while a country bus let an old woman off; then, almost at once, they turned out of the lane and bumped through an open gate and up a rutted track. The hedges were even higher here, and so tall and straggly that in places they met overhead.

Mr. Hughes laughed. "Hang on to your hats! Hope you've got your seat belts on!"

"Sorry about your springs," Ma Potter said. "Nearly there, I think. Who'd have thought it would have gone wild so quickly!"

"Been several months," Mr. Hughes said. "I did come up once or twice, thought I'd have a go with the scythe. But the years have crept up on me."

"Nature takes over," Ma Potter said, as the cab slowed and stopped outside a big house with boarded-up windows. "Before I left, the ivy was creeping into the house through the walls."

"Is this where you used to live?" Cora asked.

Ma Potter looked surprised, as if she had forgotten Cora was with her. "Yes, that's my house. Up for sale now."

"There was talk it was going for an old people's home, but that came to nothing," Mr. Hughes said. "Asking too much, so they said in the village."

"Not my doing," Ma Potter said. "She was always a greedy girl. Give me a hand, Mr. Hughes, will you? I'm as stiff as a plank."

Even with the old man's help she was awkward and

slow getting out of the cab. When she straightened up finally, her cheeks and her mouth had turned purplish. She said, "Just get my breath."

"Don't you give out on me," Mr. Hughes said. "I don't fancy carting a corpse back to your daughter."

"Who knows, she might thank you!" Ma Potter said. She looked at Cora and added, quickly, "I'm all right now. I want to show Cora the Folly."

A path led round the house; its stones covered with a low-growing plant that smelled sweet as their feet trod upon it. At the back, the grassy ground fell steeply away toward a dip in the land, a small, wooded valley, and rose again beyond the trees. Mr. Hughes held Ma Potter's elbow as they slowly descended the slope, but at the bottom she shook herself free as if she had suddenly recovered her energy. She set off at quite a fast pace into the wood, and Cora followed her.

A dirt path twisted among the trees and came down to a plashy stream with a narrow wooden bridge over it. Beyond the bridge the path led to a little glade, and there, dappled with shifting sunlight, was the smallest and prettiest house Cora had ever seen. It was a round house, built of pale, yellowish stone with arched, Gothic windows glazed with green glass, and a green door with a brass hand for a knocker. "It's like a house in a fairy tale," Cora said.

Ma Potter said, "It's called a folly because it was a piece of foolishness, built just for fun. Nowadays you would call it a summer house, I suppose, and keep garden tools in it." She opened her handbag and pulled out a key with a label attached to it and gave it to Cora. "Why don't you open it up for us?"

The key turned easily. The door opened into a tiny round room, full of green light. There was a stone bench round the walls and some dusty velvet cushions. "I used to sit here at night and listen to the nightingales," Ma Potter said.

Cora didn't much care about birdsong, but she thought she would like to live in this little house. "It's just the right size for a person," she said.

She sat on the stone bench, on a velvet cushion, and Ma Potter sat beside her. Mr. Hughes nodded at them from the doorway and said, "Back in a minute, okay?"

After he had gone, they sat for a while in a peaceful silence. Although the stone was cold, the air was warm, and the house felt friendly to Cora.

She said, "It would be a good place to hide. If you were a Cavalier running away from the Roundheads. Or a refugee in a war. Or a spy." She thought of something else. She said, "Is Angelica's father really a spy?" She had promised not to tell anyone, but Ma Potter wasn't "anyone"; she was Angelica's grandmother.

"Is that what she told you?" Ma Potter sighed a little, as if something had saddened her. Then she said, "Angelica's father sells washing machines. A more respectable occupation than being a spy, if not quite as interesting.

But you better not tell her I told you. She wouldn't forgive me." She sighed again and added, to herself it seemed, not to Cora, "Poor child."

It seemed to Cora that Angelica was not poor at all, simply a liar. So to say she was poor was a kind of humbug. She said, "You know those sweets. The ones Grandpa has. Why are they called humbugs?"

One of the things Cora liked most about Ma Potter was that if you asked her a question she always answered it properly. She said thoughtfully, after a minute, "I'm not sure. It could be that the stripes in a humbug were supposed to be made of aniseed, but because aniseed was expensive they used something cheaper. And since everyone knew this, the people who made these particular sweets called them humbugs. It was a joke everyone shared. The manufacturers and the customers."

"Grandpa says humbugs are magic," Cora said. "I used to believe him when I was young. I don't now, of course."

"I'm not sure that I'm right about the aniseed," Ma Potter said. "We'll look in the dictionary or the encyclopedia when we get home."

Except for her big, floury nose, her face had turned purplish again, Cora thought. And coming back at that moment, Mr. Hughes noticed it, too. He tapped his finger on his wristwatch and said, "Better not overdo, or you'll be for the high jump."

"Oh, just once in a while," Ma Potter protested. But she seemed ready to go, all the same, and once she had been helped back to the taxi, she settled into her seat with a little *puff* of pleasure.

Cora said, "Thank you for taking me out, it was a really super morning," and a little to her surprise, Ma Potter reached out and took her hand and held it for quite a while.

No one spoke much on the way home. There was a comfortable silence between them, as if they had all had a happy time and wanted to be quiet to remember it.

It wasn't until Mr. Hughes had dropped them at the gate and they had watched his taxi out of sight up the lane that Cora heard Ma Potter sigh. It was only a small sigh, but it was enough to tell Cora that Ma Potter felt just as she did about having to live with Aunt Sunday and Angelica. Worse, perhaps. Ma Potter had said, *a life sentence.*

It made Cora feel shaky inside. Suppose they were late for lunch. Suppose Angelica had had a nasty time with the dentist. Suppose Aunt Sunday was still feeling annoyed with Ma Potter. . . .

Cora slipped her hand under Ma Potter's arm, not to help the old lady, but to comfort herself. Ma Potter squeezed her hand with her elbow and looked down at her. She said, "Cheer up, they can't shoot us."

What they actually did, Cora thought later, was much worse than shooting. As she and Ma Potter walked up the path, the front door flew open and Angelica was there, witch-green eye flashing, and Aunt Sunday behind her, face swollen with anger.

Angelica said, "Where is it, Cora? What have you done with it? Where have you hidden the diamond ring?"

·ᕽ C H A P T E R ᕽ·

9

ora said nothing. She couldn't believe this was
happening. She could feel her ears burning.

Aunt Sunday stood in the middle of the living
room. Her face was still puffed up, a tight, balloon face.
But her voice was smooth as treacle.

She said, "Now, Cora. Listen to me. I don't want to
have to talk about this to your grandfather. Poor man,
he has enough to worry him at the moment with his sick
wife in hospital and your brother and sister to care for.
If you just give me the ring, we'll say no more about it."

Cora tried to speak. She opened her mouth and closed
it again. It was like the worst kind of dream — when
something is chasing you and you try to scream but no
sound comes out. She turned to Ma Potter, but she had
sunk into a chair, head drooping, eyes closed, as if she
were quite exhausted.

Angelica was standing by the window looking out at the garden, her back to the room. Pretending this was nothing to do with her.

Cora shook her head helplessly.

"What is that supposed to mean, may I ask?" Aunt Sunday said.

Cora found her voice. It was rough and gritty, but she could still use it. "I didn't take your ring, Aunt Sunday. I just looked at it. I looked at all the jewels. We both did, me and Angelica. We looked at them together, and then she took the jewel box upstairs."

Aunt Sunday let out her breath through her nose, like a bull snorting. "Then what has happened to my ring, Cora? What could have happened to my valuable diamond ring, in your wise opinion? Are you suggesting that it vanished into thin air? Or that my own daughter took it? Or my old mother? They have had plenty of opportunity. I have had that ring since my wedding day. Why should one of them suddenly decide to steal it as soon as a new person comes to live in the house? Don't you think it more likely that the thief was this new person? This stranger?"

Aunt Sunday paused. She stared at Cora. Then the coaxing, velvety voice was gone and Aunt Sunday shouted, "ANSWER ME, CORA!"

Behind Cora, Ma Potter muttered, "No need to use a steam hammer to crack a nut, Sunday. She's only a child."

"You keep out of this, Mother," Aunt Sunday said. But she had lowered her voice, all the same.

Cora went to stand by Ma Potter's chair. "I didn't take it," she said to her. "Honestly. I put it on, just once, just a kind of game for a minute, and then I put it back. Angelica was there, too. . . ."

As soon as she had spoken, she remembered that this wasn't true. When she tried on the ring, Angelica had been upstairs; she had gone to look for her Bible. Cora had opened the little drawer and put the ring on her finger and flashed it about. But she had been quite alone at the time.

She began to stumble and stammer. She said, "It w-was Angelica who w-wanted to look at the jewels. N-not me. I don't like jewelry much. I haven't even got any children's jewelry. Alice has some coral beads, but I haven't."

Ma Potter was watching her closely. Cora thought — She doesn't believe me!

Aunt Sunday said, speaking quietly and reasonably, "I thought you told me that you liked diamonds, Cora. You said that your mother let you wear her ring sometimes, when you went to a party. You said you wore it on your thumb."

"That wasn't true, it was just something I said." Cora couldn't explain why she had lied about this. She felt hopeless and sullen.

Aunt Sunday said, "Come here, Angelica. Come and tell us what happened. You've told me, but I want Ma Potter and Cora to hear it."

Angelica came — very slowly, dragging her feet, her

head hanging. She said, "I don't know, do I? It might have been a robber who stole the ring. Creeping into the house while we were all sleeping."

Aunt Sunday sat on an upright chair at the dining table. She put her arm round Angelica. She said, "There's my dear, loving girl. Of course you don't want to get your friend into trouble. But if we don't find my ring, then we'll have to call the police, and that will be much more unpleasant for poor little Cora, won't it, my darling? So the best thing, the *kindest* thing you can do, is persuade her to be a sensible girl and give the ring back to me."

Angelica didn't look at Cora. She said, "I went upstairs to look for something. I can't remember what it was now. Nothing important. I went to the bathroom, and when I came down Cora had shut the box up and was just sitting still on the carpet. I didn't look in the box to see if she'd taken anything. That would have been a horrible thing to do, wouldn't it? But I did think she looked a bit — I don't know — sort of *funny*."

Aunt Sunday nodded. "Then you brought the box up to my bedroom and put it on the dressing table? Did you do that immediately?"

Angelica nodded. "Then I went down again, and we went to play with our skipping ropes in the garden."

Aunt Sunday looked at Cora. She said, "I put the box in a drawer of my dressing table and locked the drawer as I always do. I didn't unlock the drawer until I was getting ready to take Angelica to the dentist this morning. And the ring wasn't there."

Ma Potter said in a distant voice, "Why should you want to dress yourself up like a Christmas tree just to take a child to the dentist? Did Angelica ask you to wear your diamond ring?"

Aunt Sunday frowned, as if she suspected Ma Potter of trying to trick her in some way. Then her face cleared and she said, "Does it matter? I canceled Angelica's dental appointment, and we searched high and low. In the chairs, under the sofa — anywhere it could have fallen by accident. I even turned out the rubbish bin in the kitchen! We emptied out my chest of drawers, and Angelica's. We didn't look through Cora's things because Angelica said it would be wrong to do that unless Cora was there." She looked at Angelica adoringly.

Cora stamped her feet, one after the other, so hard that the floor shook. "I'M NOT A THIEF. I DON'T WANT ANY HORRIBLE DIAMONDS. I DIDN'T TAKE THE STUPID RING. I THINK YOU'RE HORRIBLE AND MEAN AND DISGUSTING. YOU CAN LOOK IN MY SUITCASE AND IN MY DRAWER AND IN ALL MY POCKETS AND THEN YOU'LL HAVE TO SAY SORRY!"

Aunt Sunday had her hands over her ears and was pretending to laugh. "Dear me!" she said. "What a temper!"

Ma Potter made a noise that sounded very much like a groan.

Aunt Sunday glanced at her angrily. Then she turned to Cora. She spoke very softly. Cora thought — Like a cat purring. "All right, Cora. We'll go upstairs together this minute. And I very much hope that I shall be able to apologize to you."

Cora stumped upstairs. Aunt Sunday and Angelica were behind her, but she ignored them. She said to herself, "I. G. N. O. R. E." She had one drawer in Angelica's white painted chest, and she emptied that out on the floor. There was nothing there, just her underclothes and sweaters, and her felt pens, and her drawing block, and her recorder. She emptied the pockets of her jeans and her denim jacket, turning them inside out and adding sweet wrappers, her zipped leather purse, several screwed-up pieces of Kleenex, and a key with a label attached to it to the untidy pile on the carpet. She picked up the key and the purse and shoved them in her back pocket. Then she dragged her suitcase from beneath the bottom bunk, lifted it onto her bed, and threw back the lid.

There wasn't much in the suitcase. A plastic bag with a spare facecloth and toothbrush, an old cloth rabbit called Percy that Cora sometimes took to bed with her, and a paper bag of humbugs that Grandpa had given her and she had forgotten about. She unscrewed the neck of the bag and shook out the humbugs.

And the diamond ring winked among them.

·୬C H A P T E R ୧··

10

Cora lay on her stomach on the bottom bunk bed. Her face was buried in the pillow, her fingers were in her ears. She was blind and deaf and stiff and still, but inside her head there were demons dancing. She could *feel* them — tiny, scarlet pin men with spears poking and prodding and stinging.

She was waiting for Grandpa. She had been waiting all afternoon. He wouldn't be long now, and when he came he would put his arms round her and carry her back through the little gate, and cook her some supper. Fried eggs would be nice; two eggs, turned over quickly so that there was no more than the thinnest skin of white over the rich yellow yolk. And the yolk set just right, so that it burst when she put her fork in it.

Her stomach was making loud noises, squeaking and gurgling to remind her that she had eaten nothing since breakfast. She took her right hand away from her ear and fumbled blindly in the suitcase that was still open on the floor by the bed. She couldn't find a humbug, but she found Percy, which was some comfort. She tucked him under her chin and stuck her hand over her ear again.

She wasn't so deaf that she couldn't hear someone come in the room. Slow, heavy footsteps. Not Angelica, nor Aunt Sunday who would have spoken the moment she came through the door. "Just say you're sorry, dear, and we'll forget all about it." Or, "You don't expect me to believe that my Angel could do such a cruel thing to another little girl, do you?" Or, "Just admit you were upset and jealous and you'll feel so much better." These were the kind of idiotic things that Aunt Sunday had said — kept on saying, with a silly soft smile on her face and all the time trying to *touch* Cora, pat her or stroke her. As if she were *fond* of her, or *sorry* for her. Just as if she hadn't called her a thief!

Cora drummed her feet with rage, thudding them up and down on the bed. She said, aloud, "I would like to *kill* her. I would like to murder Angelica."

"I daresay you would," Ma Potter said. The springs creaked as she sat down. "Though easier to say it than do it, I think you may find. I've brought you some sandwiches. And a piece of Sunday's best apple cake. Not poisoned, I can assure you. And no virtue in starving."

Cora said, "I wish I was dead."

But she was too hungry to die. She rolled over and sat up and scowled at Ma Potter.

She said, "Why didn't you stick up for me? Tell Aunt Sunday what happened. That Angelica hid that ring in my suitcase. That she did it to spite me."

Cora ate two sandwiches while Ma Potter pondered in silence. At last she said, "She would have thought that I was only taking your side because I dislike my own grand-daughter. Which is true, but hard on Sunday. You can't expect her to enjoy being told that her only child is a monster. Nor, to be honest, would I enjoy telling her. And last but not least, I have to live here. Are you going to eat all those sandwiches?"

Cora shook her head. "You can have the apple cake, too. I'm full up. I expect missing lunch shrunk my stom-ach. You've got that house. Why don't you go and live *there?*"

"Too old, too tired," Ma Potter said, munching the apple cake. "I should never have left, perhaps. Mr. Hughes used to look after the garden, and he and his wife were prepared to move in. Their daughter and her family live with them, several great, noisy boys, so it would have been a kindness to them as as well as to me. Peace and quiet in exchange for keeping an eye on the old woman. But Sunday was against it, and I wasn't strong enough to stand out against her. I promised her the money when I sell Underhill. Maybe that's all she wants. Maybe she really worries about me."

She gave Cora one of her sharp, thoughtful looks. "She's worried about you," she said. "She says she's upset that you should have been so unhappy in her house."

Cora pulled her sick-cat face. "I'm not unhappy. I'm angry."

Ma Potter nodded and sighed. "Yes," she said, "I suppose you would be. Would you like me to read you a story?"

Ma Potter read to Cora out of the *Just So Stories*. Cora had asked for "The Elephant's Child," but she went to sleep in the middle and when she woke up, Ma Potter had gone.

It was after seven o'clock. Cora tumbled off the bunk bed. Grandpa usually came about seven. Terrified in case she had missed him, she hurled the bedroom door open and hit her own nose in her hurry.

Grandpa was in the living room, on the sofa with Aunt Sunday beside him. Cora rushed straight to him, her eyes full of tears from the pain in her nose. She said, choking, "Oh, *Grandpa!*"

He held her between his knees. He looked at her very seriously. Then he took out his big, red, cotton handkerchief and said, "It's all right, pet, dry your eyes, worse things happen at sea. No one's going to make you walk the plank here."

He was trying to make her laugh. But he thought she was crying because she had been caught stealing.

"I'm not *crying*," she said, outraged. "I banged my *nose*, Grandpa!"

He looked at Aunt Sunday. He raised one of his whiskery eyebrows and smiled, rather sadly.

Cora said, "My nose *hurts*. It hurts so much I think that it's broken."

Aunt Sunday leaned close to Grandpa and spoke to him softly, almost as if she thought Cora was too deaf to hear her. "Poor little girl. You mustn't be *too* angry with her. I expect she only did it becuse she was missing her mummy. And you can see that she's sorry."

Cora thought she would burst with rage. She wanted to jump up and down, scream and stamp, but Grandpa was holding her much too firmly. All she could move was her head. She jerked it about and shouted at the top of her voice, "I'M NOT SORRY, I'VE NOT DONE ANY-THING TO BE SORRY ABOUT, IT'S ANGELICA TELLING LIES, I HATE HER, SHE'S A STINKING HORRIBLE . . ."

"THAT'S ENOUGH!"

Old men can roar even louder than little girls. Grandpa's voice was full and rich like a hunting horn, or a bugle. It stopped Cora mid-yell. She gasped, her mouth open.

"Yes, I think that's quite enough," Grandpa said, returning to his usual gentle and reasonable tone. He dabbed at Cora's eyes with his red handkerchief and then held it to her nose. "Blow," he said, and she blew. Out of the corner of her eye she saw Aunt Sunday stand up and tiptoe away.

Grandpa looked up and gave a quick, satisfied nod, as if it had been arranged beforehand that Aunt Sunday should go away and leave him alone with Cora. He waited until the door closed before he put his handkerchief back in his pocket and smiled at her.

"That's better, isn't it? Now, pet, you listen to me and don't interrupt. I'm not angry with you. Just a little surprised, perhaps, but as Aunt Sunday says, you've been through a difficult time. Couldn't be helped, of course, but there we are. And all's well that ends well. Aunt Sunday thinks the best thing is to forget all about it, and that means no one else has to know. Not Granny, nor Alice, nor William. I'd like you to feel you could tell Aunt Sunday you're sorry, but that's up to you. She doesn't expect it. She's very good, Cora."

Cora was pulling her potato face. This was a solid, square, stupid face, made by puffing out her upper lip, and pulling the corners of her mouth down, and screwing her eyes into dark, tiny points, like the eyes in an old potato. It was a good sort of face for being told off for something you hadn't done.

When Grandpa had finished, she said, "What Aunt Sunday says is all humbug. I don't mean like your sweets, but saying she's sorry for me because Mum and Dad went to Japan and that made me into a thief. I don't know if *she* put the ring in my suitcase or if Angelica did. But I didn't."

Grandpa was looking doubtful. Cora thought afterward that if she hadn't gone on to say what she did, he might have begun to believe her.

But she did go on. She said, "I think it must have been Angelica. She hates me. And she's not just an ordinary horrible girl, she's a monster. That's what Ma Potter calls her. But I think she's more of a witch."

Now Grandpa was shaking his head. He said, with a little smile, "Cora, my pet, I think you must have misunderstood Mrs. Potter. She's a very old lady. And as for Angelica being a witch — well, you've always had a good imagination, haven't you? Too much, perhaps. She seems a nice little girl to me. Pretty, and with nice, girlish ways."

Cora thought — Not like me! Not like ugly, horrible Cora! That's what he's thinking!

She said angrily, "Angelica sucks up to you."

Grandpa laughed. "You're not the best of friends, I can see. I think you'd better come home with me. We'll manage all right, and I'm sure you'll pull your weight like Alice and William. I think we should have kept the three of you together in the first place. But you know your granny! She does like to organize! Even when she's just about to be carried off in an ambulance."

Cora shook her head.

"I'll explain to Aunt Sunday, pet."

"No thank you," Cora said. "I'd rather stay here."

She stared at him with her potato face. She thought she would rather stay in a dungeon, chained to a dripping wall with rats gnawing at her, than go to Grandpa's house now. She had tried to tell him the truth, and he hadn't believed her. He thought she was a thief. He wished she was a sweet little girl with pretty ways like Angelica.

And she would die rather than have to face Alice and William. Grandpa had said that he wouldn't tell them, but she would have to tell them because if she didn't they would find out somehow. And they wouldn't believe her any more than Grandpa had done because Angelica had sucked up to them, too.

In fact, no one would believe her, she suddenly realized. Except Granny, perhaps, when she came back from the hospital. And Ma Potter, of course.

"Don't look so sulky, Cora," Grandpa said. "You've been a silly girl, but you've got off very lightly. We've all made excuses for you. No one has been angry. At least you could be a bit gracious about it."

He was angry underneath, she could see. And if he really believed she had stolen the ring, he was right to be angry. It was silly of him to pretend that he wasn't.

She said, "You'll be sorry one day," and felt tears coming up in her eyes as she thought of herself lying on a couch, at death's door, her face pale as milk, and Grandpa kneeling beside her looking very old and sad and begging her to forgive him.

She saw that he didn't look very sad at the moment. Old, of course, with saggy cheeks, but not *sad*. . . .

He said, shaking his head, sighing, half smiling, "Oh, Cora, Cora! Your granny would know what to do with you but I'm afraid that I don't. Never knew how to manage your mother when she was your age. Different when she was older. Round about Alice's age we began to have sensible conversations. So there's some hope for you and me, isn't there? Come and give me a kiss, and then I must go."

Cora didn't move. She allowed him to bend and kiss her cheek. It was a very rough kiss. She said, "Grandpa, you haven't *shaved*," and he rasped one hand over his chin and patted her head with the other.

"Maybe I'll find time tomorrow," he said. "Good night, pet, sleep well, nothing's ever so bad in the mornings."

He hesitated, as if he were wondering whether to pick her up and give her a cuddle. About a quarter of Cora hoped that he would. But the rest, the other three-quarters, was too stiff and hurt. He hadn't believed her. He wished she were more like Angelica. He couldn't have a *sensible conversation* with her. He liked Alice better.

She said, "Good night, Grandpa," in a polite, faraway voice, and danced out of the room. She danced out of the back door and into the garden. Aunt Sunday and Angelica were sitting on the swing seat at the end of the lawn. They didn't see Cora, and she danced around the back of the house, singing a made-up tune under her breath.

Ma Potter was sitting on the veranda. Cora pretended not to see her. She put on her blind-girl's face, lowering her eyelids and putting her head back so that she could see through the fuzz of her eyelashes, and making her mouth droopy and mournful.

Ma Potter said, "Don't be sorry for yourself, it makes things worse."

"I. G. N. O. R. E.," Cora said in a cold voice.

"If it makes you happier," Ma Potter said.

"I'm not sorry for myself," Cora said, stumping onto

the veranda and sitting on the step, her arms folded. "It's them being sorry for *me* I can't stand. *Poor little Cora, she couldn't help stealing!* When I didn't do it to start with!"

"I know that," said Ma Potter. "What about Grandpa?"

Cora shook her head. A lump had come up in her throat.

"*She* got in first? Well, she would."

"I told him it was humbug," Cora said. "But it didn't work."

"You have to be very old or very young. Your age or mine. Maybe your Grandpa isn't old enough yet. And it's only magic for the person who says it. Clears the mind, makes things easier. Like an aspirin for pain."

"Humbug," Cora said. "Humbug. *Humbug.*" And she felt the magic flow through her, making her cooler and calmer. She smiled at Ma Potter. "All grown-ups are full of humbug," she said.

CHAPTER

11

S he was almost asleep when Angelica came to bed.
She heard Aunt Sunday say, "Good night, my
Angel."

The bedsprings creaked overhead. "Humbug," Cora
said, in quite a loud growly whisper, and the creaking
stopped. Angelica lay perfectly still.

Afraid to move, Cora thought. The magic had worked.
She went to sleep, smiling.

When she woke in the morning, her heart thumped as
she remembered. But Aunt Sunday kissed her when she
crept down for breakfast and put a dish of fried eggs on
the table that were cooked in just the way Cora liked
them.

Angelica messed her eggs about on her plate. "They're
loathsome," she said. "Yucky and slimy." Her witch eye

flashed a lighthouse warning at her mother. "You know I hate the yolk runny. It makes me think of *snot*."

"That's not a pleasant thought for a nice little girl." Aunt Sunday spoke severely, and Cora looked up from her delicious eggs with surprise.

Angelica was too astonished to speak. She turned red, pushed her plate away, and glared at the table.

"Cora likes them like that, don't you, Cora?" Aunt Sunday said. "I asked your grandpa, and that's what he told me."

Cora nodded nervously. Aunt Sunday was trying not to look at Angelica. She had *changed her mind* overnight, Cora thought. She had worked out what must have happened to her diamond ring. But she was afraid to say. She was afraid of Angelica.

Cora thought — I ought to be pleased. But she was afraid of Angelica, too. She looked at Aunt Sunday, and Aunt Sunday looked at her, and for a moment, just for a *second*, seemed to be silently saying to Cora that she was sorry.

Then, suddenly, Aunt Sunday turned an even darker red than Angelica, pushed back her chair, and stood up. She said, quickly and breathlessly, that she had to go out. She had forgotten the time. She must go straightaway. She had an important appointment. If Cora and Angelica would just clear the table and take the things to the sink, she would stack the dishwasher when she came back. . . .

By the time she had got this far, she was breathing more

easily. She said, "And keep an ear peeled for Ma Potter. She said she was going to have a bath when she'd finished her breakfast. She can manage all right, but I'm always worried in case she should slip on the wet floor. . . ."

Although Aunt Sunday sounded calmer, she was still refusing to look at Angelica. Her eyes, fixed upon Cora, were pleading. She said, "*You* don't mind, do you, dear?"

Cora thought it was almost as if she didn't know what she was doing. Didn't *understand* that she was running away from Angelica! Cora wanted to say, "I don't want to stay with Angelica any more than you do, please don't leave me alone with her," but she wasn't brave enough.

Instead she said, "I don't mind, Aunt Sunday. I can look after Ma Potter."

Angelica didn't speak as they cleared the table. Once, when she stood aside to let Cora carry a pile of plates through the doorway, she laughed at her, in a sudden, sharp, sneering way, as if she knew something that Cora didn't. Cora trembled so much that she almost dropped the plates. And when she had set them down in the kitchen, she stood still for a minute, staring into the sink, afraid to turn round. When she did, Angelica had gone.

She wasn't in the living room. She had cleared the table and swept the carpet.

She wasn't in their bedroom. She had tidied both bunks and folded Cora's pajamas and put them on top of her pillow.

She wasn't in Aunt Sunday's bedroom, either. Cora

wondered if it was Angelica who had made Aunt Sunday's bed, smoothing the pale green satin cover so there wasn't a crease in it, and laying Aunt Sunday's lacy peach-colored nightgown upon it so neatly, pinching in the waist and spreading out the skirt like a fan. Aunt Sunday's glinty silver slippers stood side by side at the foot of the bed, and Cora very nearly tiptoed into the room to try them on, but then she thought of Angelica hiding somewhere, waiting to pounce on her and accuse her of stealing them, or even just spoiling them, and closed the door quickly.

She could hear Ma Potter in the bath, splashing and singing a hymn in a deep voice. "A few more years shall roll, A few more seasons come, And we shall be with those that are, Asleep within the tomb." This must have been the only verse she knew because after that she just sang, "Po-pom-pom-pom-pom-pom, Po-pom-pom-pom-pom-pom," over and over again.

Listening, Cora decided that Angelica was unlikely to be in the bath with Ma Potter. She peeped into Ma Potter's bedroom, but she hadn't expected to find Angelica there and she didn't.

Cora went slowly downstairs. It was silly, she thought. She didn't *want* to find Angelica, so why was she looking? She could go next door and forget all about her.

But she couldn't go next door. Ma Potter was in the bath, and Cora had told Aunt Sunday she would look after her.

Angelica was *somewhere*. She must be. She couldn't have

vanished. Unless she were a witch with special disappearing powers.

Cora began to feel very peculiar. She had started to itch, as if tiny insects with delicate, tickly feet were crawling all over her skin. She kept thinking she could hear noises behind her, but when she looked over her shoulder no one was there.

There was no one in the house, she was sure, except herself and Ma Potter. Angelica must be outside. Hiding in the garden.

Cora thought — Lock the doors! There was a bolt on the front door and a big key in the brass lock of the kitchen door and a latch on the door that led to the back veranda. But a locked door would not stop a witch coming in. Cora said aloud, not believing it, "Little girls can't be witches."

She held her breath until her chest hurt. Then she pushed the door to the veranda. It creaked as it opened. She smelled the soft summer air and heard the birds singing. She said, "Where are you hiding, Angelica?"

Angelica giggled behind her. Cora turned and saw the top of her yellow head poking out from behind the opened door. She came out of her hiding place, grinning all over her face. One sparkly green eye, one a bright, freckled brown. She didn't look in the least like a witch. She didn't look dangerous.

Cora said, conversationally, "D'you know what? I know a really good joke. There's a boy at my school who's got a glass eye. Sometimes when we tease him he takes his eye out and chases us with it, and that's really scary. One morning our teacher made us all sit down and talk about his false eye and ask questions, and what I asked was, why was his glass eye a different color from his real one? And *he* said he chose it specially so he could tell which one was the eye he could see with and which one was blind."

Angelica had stopped grinning. Her face had gone dark and watchful. She said, "Where's the joke? I think that's a silly story. I don't see what's funny."

Cora doubled up laughing. She gasped, "He was *behind* his eyes, stupid! So he *knew* which one was which without looking."

Angelica shrugged her shoulders. "Oh is *that* all? Of course I realized *that*."

But Cora knew that she hadn't. She said, slyly, "Some of the people in my class didn't get the point until our teacher explained it. But they were the morons. The half-wits. The dumb clucks."

Angelica was clenching her fists. She was furious, Cora was pleased to see. But since she had claimed to understand the joke to begin with, she couldn't admit that Cora was insulting her now.

So Cora went happily on. "Loonies," she said. "Fools. Numskulls. Slow-worms. Nutters. Potty-people. Creepy-crawlies . . ."

But she had begun to run out of words, and Angelica

started to grin again. She said, in a superior voice, "You must go to a very childish school."

William had taught Cora the answer to this kind of rudeness. "Of course it's childish. It would be, wouldn't it?" Cora put on a sweet and patient expression. "Since we're all children who go there."

"I expect it's a state school," Angelica said. "Your grandparents don't even have a car, do they? So I don't suppose your parents could afford to send you to a private school. Not that they'd want to waste their money on you. They can't think you're worth it. They can't even like you very much or they wouldn't have left you."

"You're pig-ignorant," Cora said. "I suppose you're jealous because I've got a real dad and you haven't. I mean, you haven't got a dad who lives at home with you. I mean, like mine does when he's not in Japan. And that stuff about schools is just stuck-up and silly. I expect that's one reason why your school wants to get rid of you. I don't suppose they like having to put up with a girl as snobbish and stupid as you."

"They're not going to get rid of me! My mother will stop them! That's what she's doing this morning! Going to see the head teacher. And I don't care if you think I'm stuck-up and snobbish. At least I'm not a robber like you! A thief and a liar!"

Angelica was so angry she spat as she shouted. Her spit sprayed in Cora's face, and Cora stepped back. But it wasn't the spit that made her heart leap. Angelica had sounded as if she really believed what she was saying.

"You know I didn't take the ring!" Cora said. But she felt weak inside.

Angelica laughed. A cold, angry sound. She said, "You needn't bother to tell lies to *me*."

"Aunt Sunday knows," Cora said. "Your mother knows! I could tell this morning. She knows it wasn't me did it, she knows it was you! And she'll tell. . . ."

"She won't *dare*."

Cora said, "You can't stop her. You're not a witch. You can't put a spell on her."

"She's not worth a *spell*," Angelica said. "She always does what I tell her without any of that sort of stuff! She knows that if she doesn't, I'll punish her. I'm going to punish her anyway for those eggs this morning." She moved closer to Cora. Her green eye was a bright, single headlamp that was blinding Cora — hypnotizing her, as if she were a rabbit crouching and trapped by the roadside. Angelica crooned at her softly. "I'm going to punish *you* for them now."

Cora shrank back, away from that blazing eye, but Angelica shot out her hands and seized hold of her hair, a great tuft at the back of each ear, and jerked Cora's face close to hers; so close that their noses were touching.

Cora could see Angelica's green eye join on to her brown one. That would have frightened her if Angelica had not started to fight like an ordinary girl in a playground. There was nothing frightening — or not in a real, scary way — about having your hair pulled so hard that it felt like your scalp lifting off. And fighting was something that Cora was good at. Although she was lighter and smaller than most girls her age, she was wiry and strong.

Certainly she was stronger than Angelica. She found that out quite soon. She got a good grip on Angelica's neck, and Angelica let go her hair at once and tried to scrabble her hands away. She scratched with her nails and kicked with her feet, but Cora paid no attention, just braced her elbows to her side and dug her thumbs into the front of Angelica's throat.

She hissed through her teeth, "Give in, and I'll let you go." But Angelica continued to struggle, bringing her knees up and jabbing Cora painfully in the stomach, and so Cora simply squeezed her neck tighter. She said, "All right, then, I'll just kill you."

And, in that very same moment, Angelica went all floppy and loose and collapsed. She fell backward and her weight pulled Cora down with her. They fell on the edge of the veranda, Angelica's head hanging over it, and Cora lying on top of her. She still clung to Angelica's neck. It was an old trick to pretend to be dead when you were losing a fight. But when Angelica's eyes rolled up so only the whites showed, and her mouth dropped open, and her tongue stuck out, Cora was afraid that she wasn't pretending. She scrambled up and tugged at the front of Angelica's shirt, trying to lift her, whispering, "Get up, please stop foxing, Angelica." But Angelica hung limp as an old soft toy with most of the stuffing gone, and her face, which was upside down over the edge of the veranda, had turned a dark crimson color.

Cora ran indoors and upstairs. She thumped on the door of the bathroom. She shouted, "Ma Potter, you better come and do something quick. I've strangled Angelica."

·❧ C H A P T E R ❧·

12

As soon as she had said it aloud, she was terrified. She didn't wait for Ma Potter to answer. She went to the bedroom, picked up her backpack and her denim jacket, and was halfway down the stairs before Ma Potter opened the bathroom door.

She heard Ma Potter call out to her but not what she said. And she didn't stop; she was so frightened that she was even afraid of Ma Potter, who was her friend. Or had been her friend. No one would be her friend now, Cora thought.

Angelica was lying where she had left her. Cora took one look — one swift, frightened glance — and then ran from this dreadful sight, round the side of the house, through the front garden, and out through the gate. But she couldn't run from what she had seen. It was if a camera inside her head had taken a picture of Angelica lying on the veranda, head hanging loose, arms flung wide, and this picture hung in front of her eyes as she ran. A picture of Angelica, lying dead. . . .

Lying dead — *but not still!* Cora skidded to a stop on the cinder path at the side of the road. Angelica's cotton shirt had been *moving!* Up and down, as her chest rose and fell! *Had* she been breathing? Could she be certain?

Maddeningly, just as Cora was straining with her mind's eye to see the picture more clearly, it seemed to slip out of focus and fade. Screwing her eyes up, trying to concentrate, only seemed to make it grow fainter and fuzzier.

She hesitated. She looked over her shoulder. She even walked back a few paces. She stood by the hedge, near the gate but out of sight of the house, and heard Ma Potter calling.

"Cora! Cora, come back at once. Do you hear me?"

Ma Potter had been a headmistress, and she sounded like one at this moment. A headmistress calling a naughty child in from the playground. Cora thought — If Angelica was alive, she would tell me. She forgot what she had said to Ma Potter. She had just told her that she had strangled Angelica. She hadn't explained that she thought she had killed her.

Ma Potter called again. Her voice was hoarse. Then the door knocker rattled as she slammed the front door. And after that, silence.

Cora waited. She wasn't quite sure what she was waiting

for. Perhaps for Ma Potter to come looking for her. While she was waiting, she fished out her purse from the inside pocket of her denim jacket, counted the money, and found she had seven pounds and twenty-two pence. She had a pound a week pocket money; her mother and father had given her four weeks in advance when they left for Japan, and she had emptied her money box before she left home.

She sighed to herself. She had been saving up for a pinhole camera that had cost ten pounds the last time she had asked. Her mother and father had said she was too young, but she had thought that if she bought one herself and asked Grandpa to explain all about it before they came home, they would let her keep it. If Grandpa said Cora understood how to work the camera and was sensible enough not to poison herself with the developing fluid, her parents were bound to agree with him. In any case, they had only said she was too young because Alice and William had been nine years old before they had been allowed pinhole cameras, and they thought it was bad for Cora to think she was smarter than her brother and sister had been at her age.

Though, of course, she *was* smarter. And she couldn't help knowing it!

Cora thought — I wish I was stupid!

She sighed again, even more heavily. If she ran away, she wouldn't be able to afford a pinhole camera for ages. She would have to spend the money on other things. *Was* she running away?

She looked up the road and knew the answer. Aunt Sunday was turning the corner with her shopping trolley.

Cora ran. She ran away from Aunt Sunday, away from the main road, toward the pedestrian path to the station. There was no one about; the commuters had already left by this time of the morning. No one to see Cora running as fast as she could, headlong through the tunnel that went under the railway and came out near the police station.

Cora saw the blue light out of the corner of her eye and swerved in a panic; she ran across the road without looking. A mail van, braking hard, only just missed her, and an old man with a little dog in the basket of his bicycle yelled at her as his front wheel slewed sideways and the dog was thrown out. It wasn't hurt, but it made a great fuss, squealing and whimpering and holding up one tiny paw. The old man picked it up, felt the paw, and kissed it better as if the dog were a baby. He looked angrily at Cora. He said, "You might have killed Mr. Johnson."

"I'm sorry," Cora said.

"So I should think," said the old man. He was small and skinny with a sharp-nosed, rather mean little face, like the dog's. Even his voice was snappy and snarly. He said, "If you don't know how to cross a road, you shouldn't be allowed out. I've half a mind to report you at the police station."

Cora said, "I really am sorry. My granny is ill, and I was running to fetch the doctor."

She wondered if she should go on to say that her granny and grandpa didn't have a telephone, or that it was out of order, but the old man seemed to accept her explanation. He said, in a disagreeable tone, "I suppose you think your granny is more important than Mr. Johnson!"

"I suppose she is to *me*," Cora said tactfully. "Just like Mr. Johnson is more important to you!"

"Cheeky little . . ."

The old man ended with a word Cora didn't understand but she supposed must be rude because a lady who was walking past them at that moment raised her eyebrows and looked shocked. She walked on a few paces and turned back. She said, to Cora, "Is this man upsetting you, dear?"

"She's upsetting *me*, more to the point!" the man snapped. "Nearly killed Mr. Johnson, that's what! So there's no need for you to be making unpleasant suggestions! For two pins I'll have you both up in court if you don't watch your tongue."

Cora didn't wait to hear what the lady replied. She was afraid that it might turn into the kind of fight that would end with the police being called. And they would take her into the police station and lock her up in a cell with bars on the window until someone grown-up came to fetch her. And if Angelica was dead, they would never let her go. . . .

She ran. She ran down the first side street she came to. She ran until she had a stitch in her side and her legs wobbled like jelly.

She sat on a seat at a bus stop and tried to think sensibly. Once or twice, when she had been very small and angry with her mother, she had packed a little suitcase and hidden among the bushes at the bottom of the garden. It had seemed real to her at the time, but of course it had been only a kind of game, a way of making her mother feel sorry. This was different. A real running away.

And she hadn't prepared for it properly. She should have packed a change of clothes and some food and more money. She could have borrowed from Granny and Grandpa. They always emptied their pockets and purses when they had collected too many heavy coins and put pounds and fifty-pence pieces into a glass jam jar without a lid that they kept on the kitchen dresser. They wouldn't have wanted her to starve, would they? So they wouldn't have minded her borrowing some of their money.

Except that Grandpa would call it stealing, not borrowing. Since he believed that she was a thief.

And now there was an even worse name he could call her. Even if Angelica wasn't dead, she had *wanted* to kill her. So Grandpa could call her a murderer!

Cora groaned — quite loudly, just in case anyone could hear what she was thinking — and a motherly woman, who had just arrived at the bus stop, looked at her anxiously. Cora said, quickly, "I'm all right, it's just my tummy's a bit empty from not eating breakfast."

She thought of the delicious eggs Aunt Sunday had made specially for her, and felt like a traitor. She stood up and said, "I think I'll go and get some chocolate or ice cream from that shop on the corner."

It crossed Cora's mind that the woman might have some sweets in her handbag, or that she might give her something to spend at the shop so that she could save her own money for later. But all the woman said was, "The Underhill bus will be along in ten minutes, so if that's what you're waiting for you'd better keep an eye on the time."

Cora smiled and said thank you, politely, but it wasn't until she was in the shop and taking her purse from her pocket that she remembered what Ma Potter had said when Mr. Hughes had taken them out in his taxi. As a joke, Mr. Hughes had asked if they wanted to go to Buckingham Palace and Ma Potter had said, *Underhill, if you please, Mr. Hughes.*

There was something else besides her purse in the pocket; a key with a label attached to it. The writing on the label was very faint, only just readable. It said, *Underhill Folly.*

She bought two tins of sardines, a small sliced loaf, two little cartons of juice with straws attached to them, and a packet of dark chocolate. She paid for them and stowed them away in her backpack. Then she saw a big basket of red apples that were all different sizes and had bits of leaves and twigs still attached to them. She said, to the shopkeeper, "Are they all right? They look a bit wormy."

"Beauty of Bath," he said. "Straight out of my garden this morning. Not like supermarket apples, I grant you, but a good deal more flavor. Take 'em or leave them. No skin off my nose."

Cora asked for half a pound. She fiddled in her purse, pretending to be looking for change, until he waved his hand and said, "My pleasure. Didn't cost me anything. If you find any worms, bring them back. Is that your bus outside?"

The woman who had spoken to her at the bus stop was already inside the bus, sitting downstairs, at the front. Cora climbed to the top deck, where she was the only passenger. Feeling better now she knew where she was going, she hummed under her breath as the bus dipped and swayed out of the town and branches whipped at the windows when the roads narrowed. The conductor came whistling up the stairs and she said, "Single to Underhill, please." She hoped this was the right thing to say, and it must have been because he took her fifty-pence piece and gave her thirty pence back and clipped her ticket, without once stopping his whistling.

She would have liked to ask him to tell her when they got there but was afraid it might look suspicious: a girl of her age traveling alone and not knowing where she was going. So she said, just in case, "My granny lives in Underhill, and I'm going to spend the day with her."

"What's your granny's name, then?" He looked at her,

one eyebrow raised. Then he grinned in a friendly way. "It's okay, I'm not ferreting. I come from there myself, see. No one there I don't know."

Cora could feel herself beginning to blush. "Her name's Potter. She doesn't exactly live in the *village*. Just outside a bit. Up a lane. I know how to get there, but I can't quite explain it." She wished she could think of a way to stop him asking more questions. She said, "What does *ferreting* mean?"

"Just a word for being nosey. You put the ferret down a rabbit hole to look for the rabbit. You're not a country girl, are you?"

He ducked his head then, to look out of the window, and to Cora's relief pulled the cord to stop the bus. Then he winked at Cora and clattered down the stairs.

Underhill was the next stop. She recognized the church with the round tower, and the duck pond. She waited on the step for the bus to stop, and the conductor came to stand beside her and warn her against jumping off while the bus was still moving. He said, "I know what kids are, think they've got nine lives, just like cats. Only Potter I know was a schoolteacher. Taught in a school near Canterbury. Taught my brother, as a matter of fact. Used to live in Underhill House until she got too frail and her daughter took her to live with her. Now the place is all shut up, no one wants it. My mother used to give the old lady a hand, and she says it's a big old barn of a place."

Cora said, "Oh, my granny isn't *that* Potter."

The bus had almost stopped. She jumped off, turned once to smile and wave at the conductor, and then set off energetically, hoping that she looked as if she knew where she was going. She thought of all the children who ran away, whose disappearance she had read about in the paper or seen on the television, and wondered how they managed to vanish without being seen when everywhere *she* went there were people who kept talking to her and asking her questions. Perhaps, after all, she was stupid.

She hopped into the ditch as the bus swished past her and saw the conductor on the bottom deck, laughing and waving his hands about as he talked to someone she couldn't see properly; just the back of his bald head and his fat neck. She told herself that the conductor was so busy talking he probably didn't have much time for noticing and remembering.

And besides, perhaps everyone would be *glad* she had gone and wouldn't bother to go looking for her! Perhaps that was how children managed to vanish; no one wanted to find them!

She came to the track on the left-hand side of the road and saw there was an iron gate she had not noticed before, pushed open and sagging on its hinges in the hedge. In the middle of the gate there was a decoration of leaves and what looked like pineapples, and the words *Underhill House* in fancy writing.

She walked along the track. There were nuts growing in the hedges, and blackberries. She thought she would gather them later, when she had made her base camp in the Folly. There might be something inside the house, a basin, or an old saucepan. The house had been shut up and locked, but she might be able to find a way in; a window left open just enough for a small girl to creep through. She had all day to explore, no one else would come here.

She had begun to feel quite excited when she turned the last bend and saw the car outside the front door, windows winking in the sun, and heard voices calling.

·ঃ C H A P T E R ঃ··

13

The people were inside the house. Cora hid in a shrubbery of rhododendron bushes, safe in a green cave. A window opened above the porch, pushing open a tangle of ivy, and a woman with blond hair leaned out. "Come and see, Colin," she shouted. "It's a wonderful view."

Perhaps Colin came to look over her shoulder. Cora didn't see anyone else at the window, which was left open, caught in the ivy. But presently the blond woman came out of the front door with a man. They were an in-between age, Cora thought, not old, and not young. They both wore enormous, dark sunglasses. The woman said, "Oh, it's just perfect, Colin. Just what we want, isn't it? The right size! And those wonderful ceilings."

Colin said, in a hushing sort of voice, "Don't let the agent hear you, my darling."

They walked up and down in front of the house, looking up at it, and presently another man came out of the
front door and joined them.

Colin turned to him and said loudly. "Quite out of the
question. It needs too much doing to it."

"That is reflected in the price, of course," the other
man said.

Colin laughed — in a way that was meant to sound as
if he didn't believe this, Cora thought — and said, "In
any case, my wife thinks it is much too big."

"Well, the ladies always have the last word," the other
man said. "There are several smaller properties I can show
you, though nothing as reasonably priced. But if you're
really not interested . . ."

"Oh, I didn't say *that*," Colin said hastily, and it seemed
to Cora that they were playing a kind of game with
rules that they all knew. Colin and his wife were going
to buy Ma Potter's house, and the other man knew that
they were going to buy it, but no one was going to
actually say so until they had played the game for a
while.

The *Humbug Game*, Cora thought.

She watched from her rhododendron cave while they
got in the car and drove away. They had left the window
open over the porch. Cora knew that burglars often got
inside houses by climbing up drainpipes, or ivy, but she
had no head for heights. She even got dizzy going up
ladders. But if Colin and his wife had opened one window,

they might have opened another window, or even a door, somewhere else. Somewhere easier . . .

And they had. But Cora didn't find it until a bit later. She went to the Folly first and opened it up, and banged the dust out of the velvet cushions and made a bed with them on the stone bench, and took the food she had bought out of the backpack, and drank one of the cartons of juice, and ate a tin of sardines with four slices of bread. She finished off with an apple that was so crisp and fresh the juice spurted when she sunk her teeth into it. So she ate another. Then she went to look at the house.

The windows on the ground floor were all boarded up; planks nailed across on the outside. The front door was locked, and the back door, and the tall, double windows on the terrace were shuttered inside. Cora walked round the side of the house, and the creeping thyme that grew flat on the stones smelled sweet as she trod on it. There was a glass conservatory built as a lean-to on the side of the house. And the glass door was open.

There were pots of dead, withered plants. But the vine, rooted outside, had grown wild, rampaging under the glass roof, making a tangled ceiling with a few dusty bunches of black grapes hanging down. It must be like this under the sea, Cora thought; dark and cool with a weird green light flickering.

Another door, not only open but hanging loose on its hinges, led to the house itself. Cora found herself in a big room, even darker than the conservatory; all the windows shuttered and heavily curtained. In the gloom, white shapes, which were pieces of furniture covered with dust sheets, were scattered like islands.

Beyond this room was another room and beyond that, a wide hall where there was plenty of light from a window halfway up the stairs. Cora went to look out of it and saw trees and green hills rising up. She supposed this was what Colin's wife had meant by a wonderful view. But she was more interested in the house.

She climbed the rest of the way up the stairs to a broad landing with rooms leading off it: a bathroom, and bedrooms, and a room with tall bookcases that might have once been a library. Cora looked at the books that were left on the shelves, but they were all in what she thought might be Greek because of the funny shapes of the letters, and she couldn't read Greek.

She went to the bathroom and was glad to find that the water was running. She took an old tooth mug she found in the cupboard; she thought, as she hadn't got a toothbrush, she could find a bristly twig as people did in books and scoop water from the stream. There had been nothing useful left in the bedrooms; no blankets or pillows on the battered brass bedsteads, and the closets and the chests had been emptied. She had opened everything, every door, every drawer, not so much looking for anything in particular, but because she liked the smell; a pleasant, musty and dusty, lavendery smell.

She thought she should see what was left in the kitchen. If she could find a magnifying glass she could light a fire. Or an old pair of spectacles would do just as well. You held the glass so the hot sun could shine through it onto something dry, like a pile of dry leaves, until it burst into flames. She had read how to do this in William's scouting book, but she had never tried it. She thought it might be easier if she could find some matches.

The kitchen was lighter than the other rooms on the ground floor because someone had pulled away one of the planks that had been nailed over the window outside. It was a big kitchen with a wooden table in the middle, and a couch against one wall, and a cushioned basket chair in front of the old-fashioned cooking range. It was a comfortable kitchen, Cora thought. A kitchen to live in.

And someone *had been* living there.

No. Not just *had been* living. Or *used to* live. Or even *might have been* living. Someone *was* living there. Now. Cora was sure of it.

The first thing was the fire in the range. Bits of wood, used as kindling, stacked at the side, and the dead coals still warm in the grate. In fact, when Cora blew on them, she saw the ashes glow faintly; if she had had more puff, or a pair of bellows, she could have started the fire up again.

The second thing was the smell around the couch. It

wasn't a clean, sweet, shut-up smell like the smell in the cupboards and drawers in the bedrooms. It was a dirty, feet-and-armpit smell. Not a bad smell, exactly. Just a sweaty, earthy, *living* smell.

Once she had sniffed it, Cora thought she could smell it everywhere. She followed her nose into the scullery and found a cracked mug and a plate in the sink. And an old overcoat that was hanging from a nail on the scullery door was full of it; almost nothing *but* smell, Cora thought, seeing how thin and torn the coat was, the sleeves hanging in shreds.

She looked in the scullery larder. The owner of the smell and the coat had laid in provisions: half a loaf of bread, a tin of condensed milk, a carton of tea bags, a piece of cheese, and several tins of baked beans. And a tin opener lying beside the baked beans.

Cora liked baked beans. She could open sardine tins because they had keys, but she had never used an ordinary tin opener. William said that she was too young; she would only cut herself.

And it turned out that William was right. It was a very simple tin opener, the kind with a sharp point that jabbed into the top of the tin to begin with. Cora managed that part of it, but when she began to lever up the lid, she cut her hand on the jagged edge, and the blood began oozing like a string of red beads.

Someone said, "Are you all right?"

She looked up from her bleeding hand. A man stood

in the doorway. He had long, straggly hair and a gingery beard. He was wearing an old shirt and old trousers that were tied with string just below the knees, and a pair of old boots with the soles peeling off. For a moment Cora was frightened, but then she looked at him properly, not just at his clothes, but at his pale face and timid brown eyes. She saw how he shivered, how the whole of him shook and trembled, and she knew he was much more frightened of her than she was of him.

She held out her hand and said, speaking very softly and gently, "I cut my hand. Look."

He winced, as if blood upset him, and said, "Hold it under the tap."

While she did this, he disappeared for a minute and came back with a piece of rag that might once have been a white handkerchief. He said, "It doesn't look very nice, but I can assure you it's clean."

Cora held out her hand, waiting for him to bandage it. For a second or so he didn't move; then he sighed and stepped forward and tied the rag round her hand very quickly. He was careful to do this without actually touching her hand or her fingers, and the moment he had finished he shrank back, away from her, and folded his arms across his chest and tucked his hands in his armpits.

Cora thought she had never seen a grown-up so scared and shy. Although he was dirty and shabby, like a tramp or a beggar, he talked like a schoolteacher. She said, speaking very softly, as if he were a little bird she was coaxing with bread crumbs, "I was borrowing some baked beans because I was hungry. I suppose they were your baked beans. I can give you some sardines in exchange, if you like."

He didn't answer. But he smiled — just a little, as if he was pleased by her offer.

She said, "All my food is in the Folly. That's the little house by the stream. I don't live there, but I know the person it belongs to and she said I could stay there. This house belongs to her, too, and I'm sure she wouldn't mind you living here, either. But I think some people are going to buy it."

He nodded. "I saw them. I hid in the wood. I saw *you*." He smiled — properly, this time. "I saw you with the old lady before. And a man. He walked round the house. But he didn't notice my door."

Cora wondered if he had broken the lock of the conservatory door or if he had just found it open. She wondered how long he had been living in the kitchen of Ma Potter's house, but she decided she had better not ask him. She thought he was the sort of person who would be made nervous by questions.

He asked her, instead. "Is the old lady coming? Does she know where you are?"

"I've run away from home, and I'm never going back," Cora said.

She thought this would shock him, she *meant* it to shock him, but he didn't seem even surprised. He gave one of his quick, jerky nods as if he had known this all along, and as if he thought that running way from home was a perfectly normal and reasonable thing for her to do.

Cora thought he was probably the sort of person you could say anything to. Since she left Aunt Sunday's house she had tried not to think about what she had done to Angelica because it made her too frightened and miserable. Now it seemed to seize hold of her suddenly, like a real pain, and she felt she had to tell *someone*. She looked at him sideways and said, "If you come to the Folly with me and help me light a fire, I'll tell you why I ran away." He said nothing, and she added, to coax him, "And I'll share my sardines with you, if you like."

By the time he had lit the fire, a smoky fire made of pinecones and twiggy branches and some small lumps of dusty coal he had brought from the house, she had told him just about everything. He had said nothing, simply sat on his haunches, tending his little fire, poking and lifting the branches to make small, glowing caverns that he gazed into intently. He didn't look at her, and when she had finished she wondered if he had been listening. Even if he hadn't heard, she thought, she felt better because she had told him.

But he had heard her.

She said, "I *wanted* her to be dead. That's what's so awful. I mean, it wouldn't be like an *accident*."

It was almost dark now, but she could see his face in the firelight, and when he looked up, crinkling his eyes at the corners and smiling in his shy way, she knew that he understood that this was the worst thing of all.

He said, "If wishes were horses, beggars would ride. I should think Angelica might be quite hard to kill. I would guess she is a good actress."

He said nothing more for the moment. He was holding a pan of baked beans over the fire. Cora opened her second tin of sardines, squashed them up a bit, and spread them on slices of bread to make sandwiches. He had brought forks and a plate from the kitchen; when the beans had heated, he shoveled half onto the plate and gave it to Cora. He ate out of the pan himself, using his fork but still eating rather wolfishly, making a lot of noise. When he had finished the beans, he wiped the pan with several slices of bread, then belched noisily. He didn't apologize. Cora thought that he had probably been living on his own for so long that he had forgotten how to behave in company.

As if he could read her thoughts, he said suddenly, "I ran away from home several years ago. I've been trying to get back ever since. I miss my mummy and daddy."

This seemed absurd to Cora. He sounded like a little boy. But he was a grown man! She puffed her cheeks out and put her hand over her mouth to stop herself laughing.

Luckily he wasn't looking at her. He was staring into the dark trees. He said, "I've been close to it a number of times. Once I spent a night in the ditch at the end of their garden. But I always lose my nerve at the last minute."

He scratched himself under his ribs and yawned. Cora couldn't think what to say. So she passed him a sardine sandwich and said, "Excuse fingers."

They finished the sandwiches. They ate the apples and the bar of chocolate. He made tea with condensed milk and tea bags, and they shared the one mug. The moon came up and the nightingales sang and Cora began to feel pleasantly sleepy, drifting in and out of half dreams and real, dreamy sleep. She dreamed he was lifting her up and carrying her and tucking her into her bed.

She woke and found she was lying on the stone bench in the Folly with the velvet cushions beneath her. She thought — still in a half dream — that she had woken because she had heard him stamping about outside, scuffing out the fire with his feet, getting ready to leave her. But when she staggered sleepily to the door of the little house, he was still there. The fire was low now, a few snakes of flame creeping and crackling in the spent ashes, and he was just sitting and watching it. He looked up and said, "Did he wake you up, the old badger? He just came to look. See what was going on in his wood. Go back to sleep."

The next time she woke, he was gone.

This time she woke properly, starting up, her heart banging, as if something had disturbed her. She thought it might be the badger come back. She tumbled off the bench and ran to the door. He must have made up the fire because it was glowing at the center, but there was no sign of him. Then she thought she heard him. That is, she heard someone — footsteps coming down the dirt path.

It was Mr. Hughes. He stood at the edge of the glade in the moonlight. He turned round and shouted. "She's here, Liz! Panic's over!"

Who was Liz?

Mr. Hughes said, "You've got a lot to answer for, young lady."

She wondered where *he* had gone. She said *he* to herself because he had never told her his name. She wondered if Mr. Hughes had frightened him off. He would be easy to frighten, like any wild creature. She wished she had said good-bye to him.

"Do you know the trouble you've caused?" Mr. Hughes said.

She put on her potato face. Behind it, her mind was busy trying to think what to do. He would be turned out of the house if anyone knew he was there. He would be turned out, anyway, when it was sold and people had to move in. Perhaps they wouldn't come till the winter, so he would be safe until then, and in the winter they might not bother to look at the Folly. . . .

"Well, I don't know!" Mr. Hughes said. He spoke over his shoulder to someone behind him. "Girl's spaced out. Like a zombie."

Ma Potter said, "I expect you frightened her, Hughie."

She was leaning on a stick. She held out her free hand and Cora ran to take it. Ma Potter said, "What a sensible place to come. And how silly of me not to think of it earlier!"

"You didn't used to be so soft," Mr. Hughes grumbled. "Time was, you'd have had this girl shaking like a leaf on the mat in your study."

Ma Potter said, "Mr. Hughes remembers me in my prime, Cora. Before we both retired, he was my school janitor. The most valued member of my staff. And always free with his advice."

"She ought to face up to it," Mr. Hughes said. "In my opinion no one's too young for that. All the upset — what a thing for her granny to have to come home to! Let alone you getting yourself overdone."

"You have to temper the wind, Hughie," Ma Potter said. "This one is a very shorn lamb."

They were talking their private language again, Cora thought. She wanted to ask about Angelica, but she didn't dare.

She said, "Is everyone angry with me?"

Ma Potter squeezed her hand. "Worried, of course. But soon as your granny heard you had gone, she insisted on leaving the hospital, and that's been a help to your grandpa. Your granny says, *Cora's all right. That child can look after herself!* It's your sister, Alice, who's made the most fuss. Crying all day, so your grandpa says."

Alice! Alice *crying!* Cora was embarrassed. Then she thought — Why doesn't Ma Potter mention Angelica? And was instantly terrified.

She said, with a silly laugh, "D'you know what? I saw a badger scuffling about. Looking to see what I was doing in his wood."

Mr. Hughes said, "Girl's unhinged, if you want my opinion. Get her home, that's the best bet. Better put this out first, though." He stamped on the fire with his heavy boots, scattering the last of it.

Ma Potter said, "Did you light the fire, Cora?"

Cora said, without thinking, "Oh no, *he* did that. I didn't have any matches." Her voice seemed to echo back at her. She felt her stomach sink. She said, "Of course he's gone now, he's not *here*. He was just a friend I met on the bus."

Ma Potter was looking at her. Cora said, "I'll just get my backpack."

The key was on the stone bench. She left it there for him to find. She closed the door of the Folly behind her and trusted to luck that neither Ma Potter nor Mr. Hughes would think about locking it.

And neither of them did. Indeed, once in the taxi, they both seemed unusually quiet and preoccupied. Cora sat in the back with Ma Potter and leaned against her for comfort and wished that the drive would go on forever. She thought — Sailing through the dark. She said, "I'm not going back to Aunt Sunday, am I?"

"No, you're not. Nor am I. Neither of us would be welcome, I fear."

Cora felt Ma Potter's chest heave with an enormous sigh. She wanted to whisper, "Is it my fault? Did I really strangle Angelica?" but she was too afraid of the answer. So she buried her face in Ma Potter's side, snuggling up close, until Ma Potter put an arm round her.

CHAPTER

14

"Oh, my darling," Grandpa said. He met them at the door and picked Cora up and held her so tightly she thought she would break.

"Oh, Cora!" Alice and William said, both speaking together. Alice began crying and William went pink.

"Come here, my love," Granny said, from the old sofa, and Cora sat beside her, and Granny stroked her cheek and looked into her face — as if she were *learning* it, Cora thought.

It was one o'clock in the morning and no one was in bed; no one in Cora's family. And since Mr. Hughes and Ma Potter were there as well, Mr. Hughes sitting comfortably in the chair Grandpa usually sat in, and Ma Potter in Granny's rocking chair with the green, padded seat, it was almost as if they were having a party. Like Christmas, with everyone staying up past their bedtimes. But the house next door was dark; Cora had looked as they walked up the path.

Cora said, "Is your leg better, Granny?"

"Stronger than ever," Granny said. "But I intend to be more careful in future. You and I have both had a tiresome time because I fell out of that apple tree! Oh, I'm so sorry, my love."

There were tears in her eyes. Behind Cora, Grandpa blew his nose very loudly.

He said, "I suppose I'd better ring the police station."

It seemed to Cora that her heart had gone solid inside her; it was banging about like a football. She said, "Do the police know about me?"

"We had to tell them, Cora," Granny said. "When you didn't come back."

"Don't worry, pet, they won't shoot you," Grandpa said cheerfully. "Alice, would you make tea? I think we would all be grateful. Unless you would prefer beer, Mr. Hughes?"

"Whisky's my tipple," Mr. Hughes said. "But not when I'm driving."

"We should be on our way anyway, Hughie," Ma Potter said. "If your poor wife is waiting up."

She got stiffly out of the rocking chair. Grandpa hurried to help her; he put his hand under her elbow. Mr. Hughes took her other arm. Cora thought she looked a bit purple-faced and tired, but not quite so old as she used to.

She said, "Why are you going with Mr. Hughes?" As

soon as she had asked this question, she was afraid. She didn't want to be told what had happened in the dark house next door. She added, quickly, "I thought he didn't have any room where he lived. That's what you said."

"I think we can manage for tonight," Ma Potter said. "Or for what's left of tonight. We have things to talk about." She smiled at Cora. "You and I have things to talk about, too, but I think they can wait for the moment."

They left in a flurry of good-byes and good-nights, and Grandpa went with them, carrying a flashlight to see them to the taxi because it was dark on the cinder path between the gate and the road. After they had gone, Alice began making sobbing noises — or perhaps she had been making them all the time, Cora thought, and no one had noticed. Certainly, her nose was quite red.

Once she had everyone's attention, she sighed and mopped her eyes. "Oh, Cora, I'm so glad you're back. It's been so dreadful, especially for me and William! I kept thinking, what will we say to Mummy and Daddy if anything's happened to Cora? I didn't know how we could bear it."

Granny said, "Yes, Alice dear, we all know how much you have suffered. You'll feel a lot better if you do what Grandpa says and go and get us all a nice cup of tea. And a plate of biscuits. We all need to keep our strength up, I think. Why don't you help her, William?"

When they had gone, she said, "Now, Cora love. I have some idea about what's been happening. Tell me what *you* think happened. What made you run away?"

Cora looked at her grandmother. She was shivering, and her mouth had gone dry.

She said, "They said I stole a ring and I strangled Angelica."

Granny took Cora's two hands and held them. She shook her head, smiling. "Oh, what a fuss about nothing! Little girls are like magpies, they see something sparkle and of course they pick it up. The most natural thing in the world."

She was looking at Cora's hands as she spoke. Turning them over. She said, "You've got pretty hands. Delicate fingers. Just right for diamond rings when you are older."

Cora said in a husky voice, "But I didn't, Granny. I didn't *take* her ring. Ma Potter knows I didn't. And *she* knows, too. Aunt Sunday knows."

Granny looked at Cora, straight into her eyes — as if she could see through them into her brain, Cora thought. Then she gave a quick, decisive nod. "Yes," she said. "That's what I guessed, Cora."

"Grandpa thinks I took it," Cora said. "I told him I didn't. But *he* didn't believe me." Saying this gave her an ache in her chest. But there was something even more important than Grandpa thinking that she was a thief. She said, "Angelica knew I hadn't taken it. But she teased me. So we had a fight. . . ."

Granny said nothing. It seemed to Cora that she looked suddenly sad.

She thought — Perhaps Angelica really was dead and

Granny had decided not to tell her just yet. Grown-ups often hid bad things from children. Thinking like this made Cora feel dizzy, as if she had come to the edge of a precipice and looked down into space.

Granny's voice came from a long way off. "Put your head down, child. That's right, down between your knees."

Granny's hand was on the back of her neck, pressing it. Cora felt the sweat cold on her forehead.

Granny was saying — to someone else, not to Cora — "Of course, she must be exhausted."

Grandpa's voice rumbled in answer. Cora didn't hear what he said, but she felt his arms round her. Held against his chest, she felt his heart beating.

Granny said, "Put her down in that chair, Willy. It's not really long enough but it'll have to do. I want her where I can keep an eye on her tonight. I don't suppose I shall sleep much on this old sofa! We really should have pensioned it off years ago." Then her voice changed, became lighter, a little cracked, breathless. "Oh, Willy, thank God she's safe. What a nightmare it's been!"

Although she was feeling better, Cora kept her eyes closed. She had forgotten Grandpa was called Willy. It was why William's name had never been shortened: to make a distinction between him and his grandfather. And she was pleased to know Granny was glad she was home. She thought that if she kept quiet she might find out other things.

She thought — Where is Aunt Sunday? The house had

been dark. Aunt Sunday might have been in bed. Or she might have been at the hospital with Angelica. Or at the undertaker's shop. Last year, Alice had made her look into the undertaker's window whenever they went shopping with their mother. There was nothing to see in the window except a vase of flowers in front of a curtain, but Alice had promised Cora that if she kept looking, one day the curtain would be left open and she would be able to see dead bodies piled up like logs in the back of the shop.

At the time, Cora had believed her. Now she knew that Alice had only been teasing: dead people were put into coffins in the Chapel of Rest, where their friends and relations could visit them and keep them company. Aunt Sunday wouldn't leave Angelica alone in her coffin; she would sit beside her and cry. Thinking like this, seeing Angelica in her mind, lying with her pretty hair curling around her dead face and her witch-green eye closed, made Cora want to cry too. Tears oozed from under her squeezed-shut eyelids and trickled into her ears.

She heard Granny say in a hushed voice, "I think you'd better drink your tea in the kitchen, Alice, then you and William must go straight to bed. Grandpa will see to Cora and me, the poor little lass needs sleep more than anything."

Alice was murmuring something. The door closed. Granny said, with a sigh, "Just take her shoes off, Willy, don't try to undress her. Put that blanket over her and a cushion under her head — no, no, not like that, silly man, you'll give the child a stiff neck. . . ."

It was an effort for Cora to stop herself laughing as Grandpa tried to do as he had been told. He left Cora's shoes until last, and managed to wriggle them off without undoing the double knot. She half opened her eyes, and said in a pretend-sleepy voice, "Thank you, Grandpa."

He wasn't taken in. He tucked the blanket over her feet and said, in her ear, "Go to sleep, little fox."

He had spoken softly, but Granny had heard him. She said, "What did you say, Willy?"

"Just, *sleep well*," Grandpa said, with a smile in his voice. "Which is what you should be doing, my darling. You can finish your tea, but then I am going to make you comfortable and turn out the light."

Cora knew that while Grandpa guessed she was listening, nothing interesting would be said. She didn't mean to go to sleep all the same; she meant to stay awake until Grandpa had gone to bed so that she and Granny could lie awake and talk in the darkness. But while Grandpa was tidying up Granny's sofa, and fetching her a hot-water bottle, and looking for the little brass bell made in the shape of a lady in case Granny needed him in the night, Cora could feel sleep washing over her like the sea. To begin with she struggled against it, but the warm waves were too strong for her, and the last thing she heard was the sudden tinkle of the bell under the brass lady's crinoline, and Granny's soft laughter.

·◦CHAPTER◦·

15

No chance to talk to Granny next morning. When Cora woke up, she was already up and dressed and marching proudly around the room, showing off on her crutches. Cora sat up and blinked at her and she said, "Up you get, lazybones, the sun's shining."

They had breakfast in the garden, and after breakfast Granny's friends came to visit her, bringing bunches of flowers and plants in pots and boxes of chocolates and bags of detective novels until the garden seat was piled high, and Alice and William and Grandpa were kept busy supplying cups of tea and coffee and glasses of lemonade.

"It's like a birthday," Cora said, hanging about next to Granny, waiting for a quiet moment to speak to her. She thought that if she listened carefully she might find out something; someone might even mention Angelica. But all she heard was a lot of dull talk about Granny's accident and her operation, and other people's accidents and their operations. Leaning against Granny, Cora sighed with boredom, and although Granny put her arm around her, Grandpa frowned. He said, "Run along, pet, you can't always be the center of attention. It's Granny's turn now."

Cora put on her potato face but neither he nor anyone else took any notice. She stumped indoors and went upstairs to her little boxroom and looked out of the window into Angelica's garden. A man was there, cutting the grass. Cora ran downstairs and out of the door and sneaked through the little gate. The man was trundling up and down, swerving his mower in a big curve at the end of each line. Cora trotted after him, and the cut grass blew round her and stuck to her shoes. The man ignored her until he had finished the front lawn. Then he switched off the engine and said, "All right, then, what are you playing at?"

"I live next door," Cora said. "There's a girl lives here, isn't there? Same age as me."

"If you say so," the man said.

"You must know who lives here," Cora said. "Somebody must have asked you to cut the grass, I mean, it's not your grass, is it, so somebody must pay you for doing it."

"Is that so?"

"Well," Cora said, "*normally* people get paid for cutting

other people's grass. I mean that's the *normal* thing, isn't it?"

"How do you know this is someone else's grass? How d'you know it's not mine?"

Cora looked at him carefully. He had a long, thin face with a long, thin nose that quivered at the tip like a rat's. There was a brown eye on one side of his thin nose and a green eye on the other. Cora said, "Are you Angelica's father?"

George Dearheart shrugged his shoulders and sighed. Cora thought he looked sad. Frightened, she burst out, without thinking, "Is Angelica all right?"

"All right?" he said slowly. "All *right?*"

"I mean," Cora said, "I mean she's not — " She took a very deep breath. "I mean, she's not *dead?*"

George Dearheart smiled. He had two long, yellow teeth in the front of his mouth. More of a rabbit than a rat, Cora thought. He said, "She wasn't dead late last night when I met her and her mother at Waterloo station. If not being dead counts as being all right, young Angelica was quite all right then. Not that we had all that much conversation. I gave them the key to my flat, Sunday gave me the key to this house. Switcheroo."

"Switcheroo?"

"They're on the move again, so as usual old George has to up sticks until they find a more congenial place to go. The wife doesn't consult my convenience; her daughter's feelings are what count with her. There's been the usual trouble at school. Apparently they're determined not to have Angelica back this next term. So the wretched girl throws one of her tantrums and — bingo! I'm down here, cutting the grass and putting the house on the market!"

He rubbed the bridge of his long, thin nose and looked hard at Cora. He said, "The school said she frightened the other children. Did she frighten you?"

"To begin with," Cora said. "Not in the end. We had a fight and I won."

She felt light and free, as if a huge weight had been lifted from her. She hadn't killed Angelica. She hadn't even hurt her. If she had hurt her the least little bit, the tiniest bruise on her neck, Angelica would have made a terrible fuss, thrown "one of her tantrums," and Aunt Sunday would have complained to Granny and Grandpa.

Cora said, "Do you mean they're really not coming back? What about Ma Potter?"

George Dearheart laughed. He said, "Angelica will never go back to a place once she's been rumbled. And my wife had a row with her mother. The old girl finally told her a few home truths."

Cora said curiously, "What does *rumbled* mean?"

"Found out. Once Angelica's been found out for the nasty piece of work that she is."

He spoke quite calmly and casually, as if it was perfectly natural for a father to speak like that about his own little girl. But then, almost at once, he looked ashamed and uncomfortable and said, turning away from Cora, "You'd better run along, I've got a lot to do. And if you see my mother-in-law, tell her I'm here and would like a word with her."

"I didn't like him much," she said to Ma Potter. "He said something horrible about Angelica."

Ma Potter raised her eyebrows. Cora said, "I thought it was beastly of him, when she's his own little girl. Even if it would be humbug if he said he liked her when he didn't."

"Oh, humbug is not always bad," Ma Potter said. She smiled at Cora and patted her hand. They were sitting on the garden bench together. It was early afternoon, the visitors had gone, Alice and William were watching television, Grandpa was reading, and Granny was resting.

Ma Potter said, "Tell me about the friend who lit the fire for you. The friend you met on the bus."

Cora hung her head. If she told Ma Potter he was living in her house, she might tell the police and ask them to turn him out. And he would be frightened if the police came, scared of their heavy feet and their loud voices shouting. . . .

"He's not there anymore," Cora said quickly. "He just lit the fire for me and went away. I suppose he was sorry for me being all on my own. That's why he lit the fire. For company."

She could tell by Ma Potter's silence that she didn't believe her.

Cora drew a deep breath. She said, "He's not doing

anything wrong. I mean, he's not done any harm. I don't think he has anywhere else to live. He'd like to go home to his mother and father but he's too afraid. I suppose they must have been cruel to him."

"Not necessarily," Ma Potter said. "It may be just life that's been cruel. What does he look like?"

"Like a tramp. Except he's got a posh voice. And he's such a timid sort of person. It would be awful if anyone was rough with him."

"I think I can promise you no one will be," Ma Potter said. "Not as long as he stays around Underhill. Everyone knows he is harmless. When I was living there, I used to put food for him in the conservatory and leave the door open. I used to see him sometimes, in the distance, among the trees, but he would never come close."

"He only came to me because I cut my hand," Cora said. "I expect he would have come to you if you'd needed him. But the other people won't let him stay, will they? I mean if they buy your house."

She remembered that she hadn't told Ma Potter about the people she had seen at Underhill House. But there was no need to tell her because Ma Potter said, at once, in a clear, strong voice, "I'm not selling it."

She sounded pleased with herself. She said, "Hughie and his wife think they can manage. The old place is falling apart, but it'll last our time. And none of us is fussy about housework and gardening. I shall be glad to get back there. So you don't have to worry about your friend anymore."

Cora sighed. She said, "I suppose I ought to tell you. He smells *bad*. You won't want him in the house."

"He wouldn't want to be there," Ma Potter said. "There's a good loft over the old garage. I might get Hughie to make sure it's watertight. And, of course, when we're settled in, we shall be pleased if you will pay us a visit."

"Oh," Cora said. Her chest seemed to swell up with happiness. She said shyly, "I'd very much like to come. If Mum and Dad let me."

"They may not be so keen when they hear what's been happening." Ma Potter looked grim. She lifted her chin. "I feel that I owe them an apology, Cora. I certainly owe you one. I should have spoken up for you earlier. I may be old, but I'm not finished yet. I was sorry for Sunday, that was the trouble. Pity is a terrible trap."

Cora didn't understand what she meant. But she slid her hand into Ma Potter's and said, "That's all right. I mean, everything's quite all right, really."

And half an hour later it was. Grandpa had called them in for tea. Alice had made peanut butter sandwiches and egg-and-cress sandwiches and some very small honey sandwiches made of brown bread with the crusts cut off, especially for Granny.

"It's my leg that's in trouble, not my jaw or my teeth," Granny said.

But she looked at Alice lovingly and added, "You have been such a good girl. A tower of strength, Grandpa says!"

Alice blushed and simpered in a silly way that disgusted Cora. She pulled her sick-cat face and slumped on the floor.

Then the telephone rang. Alice ran to answer it. She closed the door of the living room behind her.

Grandpa said, "Nine hours difference, I think. Four o'clock here, one o'clock in Tokyo. One o'clock in the morning." He was looking at Cora. "They'll want to speak to you, pet. Last time they rang, you were next door. So they know about Granny."

They were all looking at her now. William, Granny, Grandpa, and Ma Potter. She couldn't tell what any of them were thinking. She whispered, "What shall I say?" And felt her cheeks grow hot as she thought of the terrible things she could tell them.

No one answered her. There was no time for an answer; Alice had flung open the door and was marching in, saying crossly, "Of course, it's you they want, Cora."

She walked on jelly legs to the hall and picked up the telephone. She said, "Hallo."

Her mother said, "Cora, darling. It's lovely to hear your voice, you sound so wonderfully close. As if you were in the room, not the other side of the world! Oh, we do miss you. Are you there, darling?"

"Yes," Cora said.

"Are you having a lovely time? What a nuisance about poor Granny falling out of the apple tree. Still, I daresay it was exciting for the rest of you. You made a new friend next door, so something good came out of poor Granny's accident. Did you have a nice time with — oh dear, I can't remember her name. . . ."

"Angelica," Cora said.

"Isn't that the stuff we used to put on cakes? Little green bits. Decoration. Never mind, you wouldn't know that, I don't suppose, would you? I'm glad you had a happy time with her, anyway. Make the best of things, darling. We are having a good time as well, but we couldn't enjoy ourselves if you were unhappy. Would you like to speak to Daddy? Love and kisses, my lambkin."

"Hallo, Flossie Gum-Boots," her father said.

"No one else calls me that," Cora said.

"Everything okay? Hunky-dory?"

"That's what *Grandpa* says."

"Does he? Well, I expect I caught some things from him, don't you? Anyway, all we want to know this end is that you're all well and happy."

"Yes," Cora said. "Yes. We are. I am. I had a nice time with the people next door. They've gone away, up to London, and now I'm having a nice time with Granny and Grandpa. Nothing much else has happened. Are you having a nice time?"

Her father said that they were. He blew kisses into the telephone. He said good-bye. Then Cora's mother said good-bye and blew kisses. Cora said good-bye and blew kisses, too.

She put the telephone down. She had left the door open. She stood in the doorway. They were all looking at her.

Cora looked at them all in turn — at Alice, at William, at Granny, at Grandpa.

Then she looked at Ma Potter, who smiled at her. Cora smiled back — her broadest, most beaming smile — and said, "HUMBUG."

About the Author

Nina Bawden is foremost among writers of fiction for children in the twentieth century. A reviewer in *Publishers Weekly* wrote: "I'll come right out and say it. For my money, Miss Bawden can do no wrong. Her stories are a perfect blend of humor and suspense, and that's a blend difficult to achieve." *School Library Journal* has echoed the consistent praise for her unique ability to make the reader care about her characters: "Her children . . . are distinct and drawn in depth and even the flawed, vulnerable adults arouse sympathy." She has written many well-received books for adults and children, including *The Peppermint Pig*, which was awarded the Guardian Prize for Children's Literature in England.

Nina Bawden writes about herself: "I was born in London and lived there until I was evacuated with my school to a mining valley in Wales. During the school term I lived with various miners' families and in vacations on a farm. I went from school to Somerville College, Oxford. My first novel was for adults. I started to write for children when my own children discovered a secret passage in the cellar of our house. . . ."

Ms. Bawden and her husband Austen Kark divide their time between their homes in London and Greece.

EDUCATION